FAIRYTALE LOST

A Queen City Novel (#1)

LORI HENDRICKS

Illipsium Media, LLC
Virginia Beach, VA

Illipsium Media, LLC
P.O. Box 61383
Virginia Beach, VA 23466
www.website-url.com

Book Layout ©2013 BookDesignTemplates.com

Fairytale Lost/ Lori Hendricks. -- 1st ed.
ISBN 978-0-09860984-5-1

Ever has it been that love knows not its own depth until the hour of separation.

—KAHLIL GIBRAN

1 A Spaghetti Mess

"I CAN'T BELIEVE YOU are letting this one go," Isabel repeated for the hundredth time since Emmalyn had her girlfriends meet her at a Friday evening happy hour at her favorite downtown Charlotte bar. She and her latest victim, Grant, had called their relationship quits.

"Isabel, you are not helping at all. So shut up and go get us another round of drinks. Please." That came from Em's best-friend-since-second-grade Zavia. If anyone would understand Em's plight, it would be Zavia. Isabel's frustrated sigh could be heard as she stumbled off her stool toward the bar.

Zavia sighed. "Isabel's right, Em. You really should give him another shot before you give up for good. Six months is too short a time to know if someone is forever material." She picked up her water glass and took a big gulp, choking on a piece of ice, causing Emmalyn to laugh out loud.

"He was pushy, bossy, and kinda bad in bed. What's to keep trying?" Em replied, gasping for air.

Isabel returned with three shots of tequila. It took her two tries to get the glasses on the table and three tries to get back on her stool. She grimaced, sticking out her tongue as if she'd tasted something bad. "You never said he was bad in bed. Good riddance." Isabel swung her shoulder-length, chocolate brown bob out of her face as she picked up one of the shot glasses and held it up for a toast. "If he can't curl your toes, then he's of no use and should be shot in the street," she announced.

"Here, here!" Emmalyn and Zavia picked up their shots, and the three girlfriends clinked glasses. They all downed their shots in one gulp.

"Well," Zavia started with a smile, "he was the best of the last five at least,"

Em rolled her eyes and tried to get down off her stool. "All this pointless chatter has my bladder begging for mercy. I'll be back." She carefully found her footing, proud she was smart enough to remember to switch to flats before heading off to the bar after work. Em made her way to the restroom, fairly drunk, dodging happy-hour patrons with some difficulty, and keeping part of her mind at least off not wetting herself.

After using the restroom, Em washed and dried her hands. Then she took a long look at herself in the mirror. Her hair was still pulled back into her standard tight ballerina bun, but her makeup had more or less worn off. She grabbed a towel and wiped the last of her lipstick off. Taking another glance at her light-*ish*-brown face, she made the same promise to herself that she always did when she dumped a boyfriend. "No more men." She gave herself a tight nod of encouragement.

The girl at the sink next to her made a face that meant "yeah, right."

"Seriously. I mean it. From now on, it's only sex for me, no more relationships."

"Good luck with that, though you do realize that doesn't necessarily mean no more men, just no more relationships."

Emmalyn considered the stranger's words and frowned. "You're right. Oh, well. Good thing I like cats." Em took one more look in the mirror, stuck her tongue out at herself, and followed the stranger out of the bathroom.

As Em wove her way through the crowd, she stopped cold as she saw him. His head turned slightly, and she was absolutely sure the laughing man was him. The sight was instantly sobering. She hid behind a pillar so she could watch him and see who he was with. It looked like he was out with co-workers. Em quickly, if inelegantly, ducked from behind the pillar and headed straight for the table where her friends were still debating whether or not she should have broken things off with Grant.

"Hey, we waited for you."

Em walked up to the table and quickly drank all three tequila shots that were sitting there.

"Problem?" Zavia asked, her words beginning to slur.

"Of course not!" Em answered quickly with a small belch, causing Isabel and Zavia to exchange glances.

"Okay. So what's with the bum rush of all three drinks?"

"Nothing. It's getting late, we should head out. Robert will be here soon." Em tried to pull her tote bag from under the chair, but her fingers wouldn't cooperate.

"I thought you didn't want to go home and be alone tonight." Zavia narrowed her eyes at her best friend and refused to budge.

"I'm not. I'll just stay with you tonight." Em tried to smile, but Zavia wasn't buying the story.

"Emmalyn Judith! You haven't stepped foot in my house since we got Jared that snake. Now, what is going on?" Zavia demanded.

As Em tried to come up with a plausible explanation for her behavior that would cause her friends to leave the bar, *he* walked by with his friends, heading toward the exit. Isabel and Zavia spotted Lukas at the same time and had the same shocked expression on their faces.

Isabel snapped out of the surprise first. "Holy Shit! No wonder you want to get out of here."

"Shhh! Will you keep your voice down?" whispered Em furiously.

Unfortunately, one of the men from the group recognized Isabel and turned to head their way, intent on saying hello.

"Isabel. Hey, I can't believe it's you." His abrupt change of direction alerted the rest of the group, and they all walked toward the table.

"Fuck me running," Em mumbled, though not as quietly as she thought. She grabbed her bag off the floor and tried to get away before the guys could get to the table. As per her usual luck, a waiter carrying a tray full of food was passing behind her. She yanked her bag with her full strength, launching directly into the waiter in a tackle that would make any football player proud. She knocked the waiter, all of the food, another patron, and herself to the floor. She was completely covered in spaghetti sauce and pasta, head to toe.

In her fairly drunken stupor, she tried to get her bearings, but the slippery food and flailing body parts made that impossible. Lukas reached a hand out to help Em off the floor.

"Hiya, Emmy." His booming voice and sexy smile still had the power to make her toes curl. Lukas still had the most luscious-looking lips and smooth, brown skin of any man she'd ever seen. He was perfection and danger rolled into one delicious looking man.

Mortified to her toes, she refused his help and didn't allow herself to make eye contact. After a few undignified tries, she finally got off the floor. Avoiding Lukas and the very angry waiter, she tried in vain to get the noodles and sauce off her dress and out of her hair.

"Hi," she mumbled angrily. "I suppose you can't just pretend you don't see me and keep moving in whatever direction you were going in before I took out half the bar in an ungraceful swan dive."

He covered his mouth in a vain attempt to contain his laughter. "Nope."

A couple of other waiters and waitresses came over to help clean up the mess. One handed her a bunch of napkins. Em tried to smile at her as she thanked her but couldn't get past her embarrassment. She wiped off her face and picked up her bag.

"I have to go." She looked at Isabel and Zavia and motioned toward the door. She turned on her heel and stalked off.

Stuck in their stupor, Isabel and Zavia slid off their stools, grabbed their bags, and followed her.

"It was great to see you, Brian. Um, you, too, Lukas." Isabel reached out and shook Brian's hand and ran out the door following Em and Zavia.

2 HERE WE GO AGAIN

FORGETTING ENTIRELY THAT SHE had a ride on the way, Emmalyn tried desperately to hail a cab. Every single stupid one was carrying a passenger.

"This is some bullshit," she muttered mostly to herself, as she tried to find the cellphone at the bottom of her humongous tote bag. "If I wanted to walk home, there would be a thousand fucking cabs asking me if I need a lift."

Her bag slipped off her shoulder and fell to the ground, spilling much of the contents across the sidewalk.

"That's it. I've had enough," Em yelled to the sky. Then she did something she hadn't done in almost five years—not coincidentally, the last time she saw Lukas. She crumbled to the sidewalk, broke down, and cried.

Isabel and Zavia walked out of the bar and, seeing their friend crumbled in tears, rushed over to comfort her. Zavia put her arms around Em and began rocking her back and forth, as Isabel scrambled to pick up the dropped items from Em's bag and stuff them back in.

"Please don't cry. Everything is gonna be okay. Robert will be here to pick us up in a few minutes, and we'll get away from this place." Zavia rubbed Em's back in an attempt to soothe her friend. She could only imagine how Em felt seeing Lukas again.

"Just leave her alone. She was already upset and sure as hell doesn't need you making things worse."

Em and Zavia turned when they heard Isabel's angry voice yelling a few feet away. Lukas and his friends had walked out of the bar. Lukas was trying to walk in the direction where Em and Zavia were sitting on the ground, but Isabel had placed herself between them. The view was almost laughable. Lukas was almost a foot taller than Isabel's five-foot-five frame.

"Look, Isabel, I just want to make sure she's okay. I didn't mean to upset her. I didn't even know she'd be here." Lukas peered around Isabel to Em but didn't try to get any closer.

"Whatever you think you need to say doesn't matter. Just stay away from her. She doesn't need you!" Isabel began trying to push Lukas toward his friends.

Brian took pity on her and the situation and grabbed Lukas's arm.

"Come on man. Let's just get out of here," said Brian with a half smile of empathy.

Lukas took one last look at Emmalyn sitting on the ground, crying her eyes out because of him, yet again. He started to take a step toward his Emmy but then thought better of it. Their relationship had ended in a very similar scene—the woman he had loved more than his next breath in a mass of tears and pain because of him and his thoughtlessness. He hated always being the source of Emmalyn's pain. He turned slowly and walked away from the sound of her crying, unable to fix the mess he'd unwittingly created.

Isabel watched him turn away and shot Brian a sad smile in thanks. As she turned back toward Em and Zavia, she saw Zavia's husband pulling Em off the ground. They piled her in the backseat of Robert's big, black SUV. Isabel grabbed Em's bag and jumped in after her.

"What the hell happened? Was that Lukas? And finally, and perhaps I should have started with this one, why is Em covered in what appears to be and smells like marinara sauce?" Robert pulled away from the curb and immediately launched into questioning his wife and her friends.

Zavia touched his arm and gave him a look that said "I'll tell you later."

"Okay, where are we going?" he asked cautiously.

"Home," Zavia replied.

Em finally pulled her head up off the backseat, where Isabel had been rubbing her hair and back. "No, please, take me home," she said with a hiccup.

"Absolutely not. I'm not leaving you alone tonight."

"I can't go to your house if Stanley is still there." Em looks at Zavia in the rearview mirror with a crooked half smile.

Robert laughed. "Buying that snake was the best money I ever spent. No more girl's night at my house."

Zavia punched his arm, then softened the blow with a smile. "Hush up, you."

"She can come home with me." Isabel pulled Em into a hug, and Em leaned into her. Zavia looked on worriedly from the front passenger seat. Em hated hugs, hugging, and huggers.

"She must be a total mess," Zavia thought.

"If I may, I think I have a solution. Why don't you all go stay at Em's? She doesn't have a snake like we do, and she doesn't live in a closet like you do, Isabel," Robert suggested.

Isabel made a face at the back of Robert's head. She turned to Em and asked, "Would that be better? I can grab some stuff and come by your house."

Em really wanted to be alone. She had never been so embarrassed in her life. She just wanted to crawl under the bed and die. As she replayed the scene at the bar in her head, she began to tear up again.

"You sure you don't mind if I stay with Emmalyn tonight?" Zavia gave another worried glance to the backseat, then looked back at her husband. "Obviously, something is going on. I don't think I've ever seen Em cry in all the years I've known her. Clearly, she needs you."

"No, Zee, go home. Isabel and I will be fine." Em knew how much Zavia and Robert hated being apart for longer than eight hours. She'd always wished she could find what her best friend had in Robert, but it never seemed to happen. She once thought it would, but….

Putting that thought out of her head, she tried to pull herself together as they neared the front of Isabel's building.

"Isabel, go ahead and grab your stuff," Robert instructed. "Then we'll drop you two at Em's."

Em patted Robert's shoulder as Isabel jumped out of the truck. "Thanks Robbie. I really appreciate you being so understanding." Em watched Isabel run up the stairs of her building and disappear behind the building's huge glass doors.

"I fully expect my understanding to be rewarded." Robert looked a Zavia and wiggled his eyebrows, causing Zavia to roll her eyes and smile.

"Okay, see, now I think I'm going to be sick." Em finally smiled.

Robert turned to Emmalyn, concern written all over the deep frown in his forehead. "Are you okay? You want me to kick his ass?"

Zavia, Robert, and Emmalyn grew up together, the threesome meeting in the second grade when Em's mother moved the family to the Charlotte suburbs shortly after divorcing Em's father. Robert had had a crush on Zavia for as long as any of them could remember. For Zavia, though, it wasn't love at first sight because she didn't want the boy next door, but as they all got older and entered high school, and then college, she realized he was always the one for her. Robert's tenth-grade growth spurt that included facial hair and muscles didn't hurt either. They married right after college and had their son, Jared, five years later.

"Robbie, not to be mean, but I'm pretty sure he'd pummel you." Em smiled at him, a full smile, to soften the blow.

"He may be bigger than me and work out and all that, but I'm scrappy." He flexed his skinny arm muscles, causing both women to burst out in laughter.

"Of course you are sweetie. I don't think any fighting is necessary. What happened at the restaurant was just... an unfortunate series of events."

"Yup, just call me Lemony Snickett," said Em, sarcastically, from the backseat.

"Emmalyn, I can't imagine what you're feeling right now. I know how much you loved him, but you did the right thing then."

"Oh really? How can you be so sure?"

"Because I told you to do it. That's how. And we can all agree I'm always right." Zavia smiled at her friend and tried not to remember the frighteningly dark period Em went through when she and Lukas broke up five years ago.

Em had always struggled with bouts of depression—especially after her father's death. After Lukas left, she wasn't much more than a ghost—going to work and home, never stopping anywhere or going out, for almost a year. Em was always so afraid that she'd run into Lukas that she stopped going anywhere they'd ever been together, going so far as to have her groceries delivered. She slept if she wasn't working, and it seemed as though she'd never break out of the gloom that surrounded her. During that time, Lukas was transferred to an office on the other side of the country, and Zavia and Isabel were finally able to coax Em out of her funk.

Zavia did not want to go through that again. She needed to talk to Isabel before they took Em home.

"I'm going to run upstairs and see what is taking Isabel so long." Zavia jumped out of the truck before either Robert or Em could respond.

"That was random," Robert remarked before going back to scrolling through emails on his phone.

Em smiled at Robert. He really had no clue. "Not really. Zavia is going upstairs to tell Isabel what I should and should not be allowed to do over the next forty-eight hours."

Robert paused but didn't look up from his phone. "You're not going to go after them are you?" He finally looked over at Em, who had a bemused look on her face.

"Nope. I know better than to try and stop Zee when she is in mothering mode. Besides, I'm not really in any position to argue that I can take of myself, am I?"

ZAVIA REACHED ISABEL'S DOOR and knocked twice in rapid succession as she walked in. Isabel's apartment was a fashion disaster area. She was the only one of the three friends that was what society and the fashion industry deemed "normal sized," with Zavia being too tall and Em being too hippy. Isabel bought clothes constantly and judging from the disaster area that used to be a living room, she'd finally given up trying to get the clothes in any semblance of order.

"Jesus Zee, what took you so long? I've been waiting for you!"

"Sorry. After what happened, my brain isn't functioning right." Zavia moved a stack of tee-shirts aside to sit down on the sofa.

Isabel was pacing the tiny room. "When did he get back into town? I thought he promised to let one of us know if he came back." She too remembered the mess of a woman left behind when Lukas left town before.

"I know. This is a disaster. We can't let Emmalyn get wrapped up in him and his bullshit again. I don't think any of us can take it." Zavia held her head in her hands and grimaced.

"Agreed. I'll stay with her for the weekend. Hopefully, by Monday she'll be okay again." Plan established, Isabel grabbed a bright pink designer tote bag and stuffed clothes and shoes inside.

"Good. I'll be over tomorrow after Jared's football game, and we'll keep her busy. Somehow." Zavia rose from the sofa to look out the window and started biting her nails. Isabel reached out and smacked her hand.

"Stop that," Isabel admonished. "One basket case is all I can handle at a time. You'll go home, fuck your husband, and be okay. Keep yourself together."

Zavia glared at Isabel but accepted that what she said was true. And she had every intention of thanking Robert properly and reminding him how much she really loved him as soon as Jared went to bed.

"Fine. You've made your point. Let's go before they come up here." The two turned and headed for the door. As Isabel locked her door, Zavia spoke up.

"Under no circumstances is Lukas allowed near Em. He'll kill her. She won't be able to fight him off and she'll get sucked under again. I don't see how he'll know where she lives now, but just in case, call the police if you have to. They do not need to talk or anything else."

Isabel nodded. "All right. This should be fun," she sighed as she and Zavia headed down her long hallway towards the elevator bank.

ROBERT DROPPED THE FRIENDS off at Em's townhouse just outside of the city. Hers was a three-story end unit with a two-car garage on the lower level. Em had been so proud of herself when she'd bought the house.

They went inside and ordered food, giving Em time to wash the pasta sauce out of her hair and off her body before changing into clean clothes. Rejoining Isabel in the kitchen, Em went straight to the refrigerator, grabbing a bottle of wine and two glasses from the cabinet.

"Don't you think you've had enough to drink?" Isabel walked around the big granite island with a concerned look on her face.

"Nope. Not even close." Em poured one glass half full and drank the wine down in one swallow. She didn't hesitate before pouring another.

"Well, then at least drink tequila. Mixing alcohols will just make you sick and hung over." Isabel hustled into the living room and grabbed the bottle of tequila off the bar. She headed back to the kitchen quickly and deposited the tequila on the counter. She then grabbed the wine glass out of Em's hand and the wine bottle off the counter.

"You're the boss." Em turned back to the cabinet and grabbed two shot glasses.

"Look, now, no more for me until after we eat."

"Have it your way. I just want my brain to stop churning." She poured a shot in each glass, took the first one, and threw the amber liquid back. She did the same with Isabel's.

"Em...," Isabel put her hand over Em's and searched her mind for the right thing to say.

"I'm not going to bother saying I'm fine because we both know that would be a lie." Em walked into the living room and dropped, face first, onto the sofa. "Want to hear the saddest truth of my entire existence?"

Isabel laid back on the chaise across from Em. "Sure."

"I now understand why no men I date can survive beyond six months," Em said sadly.

"Really?" Isabel really didn't like where this was going, but she sensed Em needed to get this off her chest.

"Yup. They aren't him. They are all like him in some way, but they aren't him. And after six months of trying to mold them into him and realizing it's never going to happen, I dump them. How pathetic is that?"

"It's not that pathetic."

Em turned her head and looked at her friend, hopeful that the other woman held some answers. Isabel tried to smile, to find some way of reassuring Em but couldn't quite muster it.

"Isabel, for as long as I've known you, you have said that it's wrong to sugarcoat the truth. Why start now?" She turned her head around and tried to bury her face in the sofa cushions.

"Because you are hurting, and right now, the harsh truth isn't what you need. Tomorrow I'll tell you all about the kind of idiot you are."

Em laughed at that. She turned her head back toward Isabel. "I know you and Zavia are scared I am going to go running back to him. And while I can't say it's never going to happen, I can say it's certainly not what I want."

"That's good to hear. And you're right—we are very scared of that happening. After last time, let's just say we have every right to be concerned." Isabel sat up in the chair and gave Em her serious face. "Okay, so what do you want to do tonight?"

"I don't care. Don't you have any ideas?" Em flipped over on her side and pulled her knees up to her chest.

"Of course." Isabel jumped off the chaise and ran to her bag in the kitchen. She came back holding DVDs. "We are going old new school — *Doctor Who* marathon! I just love nine."

"You are such a nerd," Em laughed. "Besides, anyone with half-a-grain of sense knows eleven is the best."

Isabel picked up a pillow and hit Em lightly across the shoulder. "Whatever. I notice you didn't say no."

"Shut up, and put the disc in," Em mumbled, refusing to make eye contact. The two old friends laughed and settled in for several hours of sci-fi TV watching.

3 THE BEGINNING & END

ALL THROUGH HIGH SCHOOL, Em and Zavia knew they'd be going to college together. When the time finally came, they got rooms in the same dorm, just three doors from each other. They briefly considered rooming together, but with Em being just shy of a total disaster and Zavia being slightly obsessive compulsive, both knew that would be a terrible idea.

The college years seemed to fly by. Once senior year rolled around, the girls wanted to move off-campus and decided an apartment would be okay—Em had to promise not to junk up the public spaces, and Zavia had to promise not to clean Em's room when she wasn't home.

Zavia had always known that she wanted to be an interior designer when she grew up. As graduation neared, she was fielding several offers from design houses all along the east coast. Em never understood why Zavia studied civil engineering if she wanted to pick wallpaper for a living, but Zavia was always one with a plan.

Em, on the other hand, flew through college by the seat of her pants. She changed majors four times in two years then had to go to summer school to graduate with Zavia once she'd decided on computer science. She didn't have a burning passion for the subject, but the subject was interesting and related careers paid well right out of college.

While in those CS courses, she'd met Lukas, who wasn't a student at the university, but rather a local that worked in the computer lab. He would always flirt with her when she came to use the computers, and she found him to be attractive and funny. She finally got the nerve to ask him to coffee on campus, but he told her he couldn't because dating students was against university regulations for staff.

The day after graduation, as Em and Zavia were packing up their apartment, Lukas stopped by and asked Em if the offer for coffee was still open. She jumped up and wiped her hands on her pants.

"Hi! Of course." She paused. "How did you know where I live?"

Lukas had the most adorable sheepish smile when he replied that his sister lived in the building, and he had seen Em once while he was there visiting. "I've avoided the building since that day so you wouldn't think I was some creep stalker."

They went to coffee later that day. Zavia and Robert were busy finalizing plans for their wedding, so Em didn't feel too guilty leaving the apartment half packed. Coffee easily turned into dinner. They talked for hours about any number of subjects.

"Why didn't you ever go to college? You seem smart enough," she blurted out, blushing in shame at the politically incorrect question.

"I went into the Army right after high school. I got injured pretty bad during a deployment. It took me a couple of years to be able to walk and regain the use of my right hand. After that, the thought of sitting in a classroom just made me crazy."

"Oh my goodness," Em exclaimed. "I never would have guessed."

"Would either of you like something else? I am about to go off duty, so I'd like to close your ticket, if you don't mind." The waitress seemed impatient to be off, so they paid their bill and left the restaurant.

"I'll walk you home." Lukas reached out and took Em's hand. Their hands touched, and alarms went off in Em's head. She'd never had such a strong reaction with anyone else she'd dated before. She looked up at

Lukas and noticed he had the same stunned look on his face.

When they reached her door, he leaned down and gently kissed her on the lips. Though brief, the kiss was powerful and intense. Emmalyn was totally breathless. She also couldn't force herself to walk inside the apartment. They stood staring at each other until the apartment door was yanked open by a furious Zavia.

"Where the hell have you been? I've been calling you non-stop, but of course you'd never know that since you left your damn phone here. I don't know why you bother paying for the damn thing since you *never* have it on you!" Zavia's lecture cut off abruptly when she noticed neither Em nor Lukas had been paying her the least bit of attention.

"Hello!" Zavia reached out and pinched Em's arm. Em reluctantly pulled her eyes away from Lukas and frowned at her friend.

"Ouch! What's that all about?" asked Em, rubbing the sore spot on her arm.

"Are you shitting me right now? I've been worried sick about what could have happened to you. Damn it all Emmalyn Judith!" Zavia snarled, her eyes shifting back and forth between her friend and the complete stranger she'd worried had likely sold Em into slavery hours ago.

"Why didn't you just call me?" Em began patting her pockets then looking in her purse for her phone. Zavia held it up for her to see.

"Looking for this? You left here without your phone. Again."

"I'm sorry, Zee."

In response to Em's lame apology, Zavia turned back into the apartment and slammed the door behind her.

Em flinched. "I better go after her. Thanks for coffee and dinner. I really enjoyed being with you today." She stood rooted in place, smiling like an idiot. She didn't care. Lukas had the same ridiculous grin.

"When are you leaving town? I'd like to see you again."

"Day after tomorrow. Zee is getting married Saturday morning, then after the reception, I'm moving into the city for my new job." Emmalyn had a hard time focusing with Lukas's thumbs rubbing circles in her palms.

"Okay. So, how about dinner tomorrow?"

"I can't. The rehearsal dinner is tomorrow. But we can meet after that. We're having the bachelorette party tonight. Zee doesn't want to be hung over for the wedding."

"Okay. I'll be waiting." He kissed her again, just as lightly, just as powerfully. He laid a finger on her cheek before walking down the hall away from the apartment. She watched him leave the building, not able to move until he was in his car and driving away.

Zavia opened the door again. "You're an idiot."

Em's smile faltered just a bit as she turned to her very best friend in the world.

"I'm in love!" She gave her friend a huge, goofy grin as she stepped into the apartment.

Zavia groaned, having heard this before. Many times. "Just tell me you didn't sleep with him."

"What? Of course not. But he did kiss me. Twice. We just shared the most amazing kiss in the history of inter-lip relations."

Zavia rolled her eyes and went back to packing books. She frowned when she realized Emmalyn was still standing in the doorway. "You do plan to help at some point tonight, right?"

"Yes, Master!" Em walked into the room with her arms out like a zombie. Zavia burst into laughter and threw the tape at her.

"Bitch!"

Em joined in the laughter and the two friends continued to prepare for the next stage of their lives.

THE NEXT COUPLE OF months passed quickly. Emmalyn and Lukas grew closer, seeing each other every weekend. The first time they slept together, Em was absolutely sure she had found her soul mate. Everything about the experience was perfect. Though she had been able to bring herself to orgasm for some time, Lukas was the first man to be able to, and he brought her intense pleasure many times that night. He knew exactly how to touch her, kiss her, hold her. He instinctively understood what her body needed and was able to give her that and so much more.

And she found ways to please him that no other woman had. Every part of her melded perfectly with his, as if made just for him. He felt so incredibly lucky to have found someone that was so compatible with him, and didn't feel the need to be false or misleading.

The first time Lukas told Em he loved her was on their six-month anniversary. They were out to dinner, and he had presented her with a beautiful pair of pearl earrings. She was putting them in her ears when his words shocked her into absolute stillness.

"This can't be a surprise to you, Em," he laughed. "I mean, you had to know how I feel about you."

"I did know. I just wasn't sure if it was real or if I just really wanted it to be. I love you too. I think I've always known."

"Thank God." Lukas leaned back in his chair and wiped his forehead with the back of his hand. "I'll admit I was a little worried by the look on your face."

"I just wasn't expecting you to say that so soon. It's been a perfect night. Let's get out of here."

That night they made love over and over. Lukas took Em in just about every way possible, the depth of their love displayed in every kiss, every caress, and every stroke. Just when Em felt she wouldn't be able to take another breath, Lukas was able to find another sensitive place and get her going all over again. Em wanted the night to go on forever. She loved the man and loved every orgasm he gave her. Eventually, she fell asleep, fully sated, against Lukas's chest, dreaming of their wedding day and the house full of kids they were going to have.

The relationship wasn't always a bed of roses, though. Emmalyn was exacting and had a tendency to be somewhat intolerant of faults in others. She expected perfection in herself and pushed hard to succeed in her career. Lukas was the exact opposite. While he worked hard for what he wanted, he was happy where he was and preferred to run his life as the situations occurred. He had very little patience for Em's planning and tended to break plans with no notice. Lukas's seat-of-the-pants attitude drove Em crazy. The majority of their fights were because Lukas broke his word to Em, not showing when he said he would but mostly breaking or changing plans at the last minute.

There were times when Em felt that if Lukas really loved her as he said he did, he'd be able to keep his word. Lukas, on the other hand, felt that Em put too many restrictions on him with her incessant planning and wished she would relax and enjoy life more. What he couldn't see was that with each broken promise and each missed date, he was pushing her further and further away.

Their worst and final fight came the night Lukas missed Em's promotion party. His father needed help moving furniture, and he'd stopped there first to give his old man a hand. He and his father ended up talking so long that by the time he made his way to the restaurant where the party was held, Em was gone. Isabel had told him that Emmalyn had left the restaurant more than an hour before, crying. Lukas felt terrible, but he really didn't think the situation was that big a deal. His pops needed him. Surely, that took precedent over some work party, right? By that point, he was no longer so sure.

He walked slowly into the apartment carrying the flowers and present he'd bought for her. As he crossed the threshold, he stumbled, tripping over something large in the darkness of the foyer. He flipped on the light to find a pair of large suitcases. He didn't recognize them, but he didn't think that was a good sign. He dropped his head to his chest and took a deep breath, steeling himself before walking into the fight he knew was waiting for him. He found Emmalyn sitting at the dining room table eating an entire round cake with a glass of wine. She wasn't crying, and she didn't look upset. Perhaps fortune was smiling on him— except for the suitcases in the hall. This was Em's apartment, so obviously she wasn't leaving.

She finally spoke, her voice calm and clear and devoid of any emotion, bringing Lukas out of his musing. "Those are your bags in the hallway. I took the liberty of stopping on the way home and picking up the bags since you didn't have any here and you sure as hell aren't taking any of mine. Now, get out." She lifted the wine glass and took a long drink.

"Em, wait a minute. Let's talk about this," Lukas said desperately. This wasn't like any other fight they'd had, and he'd grossly misjudged the situation.

Em rose from her seat and glared at Lukas. The look in her eyes scared him. He'd never seen her, or anyone for that matter, that angry. The look was so intense he didn't notice that she had picked up the plate with the cake, didn't notice the movement, in fact, until she had thrown the plate at his head. He tried to duck, but the plate caught him on his ear and broke. Cake and blood went everywhere.

"I have absolutely nothing to say to you. *Get out, now!*" she bellowed.

"Em, I was with Pop. He needed me," Lukas tried to explain.

"I. Needed. You!" Em took a couple of deep breaths and calmed her voice. Calming the storm in her heart, however, could take much, much longer. "What did he need that was so important that you would miss today? You, of all people, should know how hard I worked for that promotion. I told everyone how you'd be there. And I sat there waiting, like an idiot. Just like I always do."

Lukas tried to move closer to her. He knew if he could just pull her into his arms, he would make her see reason. She knew this as well. As soon as he took a step, she grabbed the wine glass and broke it against the table. Wine and glass flew everywhere.

"Emmy, please. I don't want to go, please." He realized he didn't care if she cut him. Losing her would be worse than any cut. He took another step toward her. Instead of swiping at him, she held the broken glass to her wrist.

"I swear if you come any closer to me, I'll cut myself." Em knew well enough that Lukas wouldn't care what she did to him, but he'd never let her hurt herself. She hated herself for doing this and for the weakness in her that wanted to just forget everything and run into those arms that had held her so many nights.

"God damn it, Emmalyn, this is not funny." He'd never known Emmalyn to act so irrationally. Just the opposite, she was always too rational, too linear. He wanted to kick himself for pushing her that far.

"I know it's not, and I'm not joking. You really don't see what you've done, do you? Let me shed some light on the subject for you. Do you remember the first night we were together?"

"Of course I do. You know I do."

"I remember that conversation like it just happened. I wanted to lie there with you forever. You asked me what my deal breakers were. Remember what I said?" she asked too calmly for someone holding broken glass to her own wrist.

He did, and as his mind registered the severity of his situation, he took a step back and slid down the wall onto the floor.

"Oh c'mon, Lukas, what did I say? You're the one always saying how you remember every conversation we've ever had." She waited for him to speak, growing increasingly frustrated. "*What did I say?*"

"You said that you couldn't abide a man who couldn't keep his promises. That I could tell you anything and that even if you didn't agree or wasn't happy with what I said, you'd respect it because I respected you enough to be up front. But Em, I didn't break...," he said weakly, unable to finish the sentence. He tasted the lie as the words formed.

"Ah, but you did. Before you left, I asked you if you were going to come to the office for the partnership ceremony then to the party, and you said, and I quote, 'I will be there, I promise, wearing your favorite tie,'" she sneered.

"But Em, you can't end a relationship because I missed one event. That just can't happen," Lukas whispered.

"Think back, my love. How many times have we made plans in the last six weeks and you either didn't show or came so late that you may as well have not shown at all?"

"Emmy..."

"I've been putting up with this for so long, I've lost count. Dinners, drinks, appointments — and a part of me breaks every time. But I kept telling myself that we love each other and you'd come to see how important those things are to me and you'd show up. But then you don't, and I break all over again. You tell me every day that you love me, but it's very rare that you care enough to show me. Your words don't matter to me, Lukas. Never did. When you bought me the earrings, you thought that I needed the words to know how you felt, but I didn't. I'd been eyeing those earrings for months, and you'd noticed and bought them for me. That's how I knew. But I need you to be there for the little things. And I didn't get the promotion by the way. They gave that job to Greg Harper. The party was for him."

Lukas felt his stomach drop. There it was—the reason this was so bad. He could hear the door closing on his relationship with Emmy, just as loud as the ticking of the mantle clock. "Oh Emmy, I am so sorry. I know how much that meant to you." Lukas started to get up off the floor, but one look at Emmalyn's furious face stilled his movements.

"I need for you to leave Lukas. I can't keep doing this with you. I can't depend on you to be there when I need you, and that's the single most important thing to me. I told you that. We both know I'll keep taking you back because I love you with all my heart. But so much disappointment—I can't function." Her eyes welled up, but the tears didn't fall. "So please, if you care for me at all, just go. Don't look back, don't say goodbye, just walk out the door."

The glass shard dropped from her hand as she slumped into her chair and put her head on the table. She didn't begin to cry until she heard the front door close.

Fast Cars & Late Nights

"SO. YOU WANT TO tell me what that was all about?" Brian looked over at the large, muscular black man erratically driving the car fifteen miles over the speed limit through downtown and wondered if he would be able to overpower him and take control of the car. He knew he couldn't and decided to try to talk him into slowing down before they both ended up in jail or dead. "Okay, then. How do you know Emmalyn and Isabel?"

"I don't want to talk about them," Lukas responded through gritted teeth. He mashed his foot on the gas, increasing his speed another five miles per hour. Brian looked around for cops and a way out, just in case.

"That's fine. Can I drive then?" Brian tried asking casually, but the erratic speeds were causing him serious concern.

"Why? What's wrong with the way I am driving?" Lukas challenged.

"Nothing—if we were racing in the Daytona 500, but since we're just in downtown Charlotte, going significantly less than seventy-five miles per hour is more appropriate."

Lukas looked down at the speedometer. He pulled his foot off the gas and let the car slow down. They rode the rest of the way to Brian's house in strained silence.

"Do you want to come in? I'm willing to listen if you want to talk. I have beer. Or something stronger." Brian tried to get his friend and co-worker to come in and stay off the roads while he was so upset.

"No thanks. I'm okay. Really." Lukas tried to reassure his friend but failed miserably. He exhaled sharply and punched the steering wheel in frustration. "Em and I used to date. I haven't seen her in five years, since the day we broke up."

"Ah, I understand now."

"I was so in love with her. I'd have done anything in the world to be with her except the one thing she asked of me. I didn't take her or our relationship seriously, and I lost her. Seeing her tonight, I just—I don't know."

"You can't still love her? A long time has passed, man, not to mention you are engaged to another woman."

"I don't know what I feel. And I remember that I am engaged to someone else. It's just that I saw her lying there covered in pasta sauce looking absolutely adorable, and I don't know... I would have sworn no time had passed, and she was still my Emmy." Brian started to laugh. "What's so funny?"

"She hates to be called Emmy. I once watched her lay into a guy at a bar who called her Emmy, and he still avoids her like the plague. I couldn't really understand why, but now I understand." Brian tried to straighten up his face. He really wasn't trying to be unsympathetic to his friend. He cleared his throat then said, "Sorry, you were saying?"

Lukas sighed. "I called her Emmy when we were together. She and I were an instant thing. I knew she was the one for me the moment I laid eyes on her." Lukas laid his head back on the headrest and closed his eyes.

"I'm sorry, but I don't think there is an issue here. She didn't seem happy to see you. Besides, you're only here for a couple of weeks then it's back to the west coast. I need a beer. If you're sure you don't want to come in..." Brian stepped out of the car then leaned into the window.

LORI HENDRICKS

"I'm sure. I need to check in with Pop, then get some sleep. We have an early start tomorrow. Thanks for listening. G'night, man."

Lukas pulled away from the curb and headed to his father's house. Driving across town, Lukas thought back to his run-in with Emmalyn. She looked exactly as she had the last time he saw her. The last five years had done nothing to diminish her beauty, at least in his eyes. He hated himself for being the cause of her pain—yet again. He knew in is gut that if only he'd had a chance to talk to her, then…. Then what? Brian was right. He was engaged to a wonderful woman back west, and he had no business trying to explain anything to Emmy. The fact was she'd thrown him out. He didn't owe her anything.

He parked in front of his pop's house and used his key to get in the door.

"Who's there?" came the gravelly voice he'd known all his life.

"No one, Pop. That's why I used the key." Dropping his stuff on the table, he walked back to the family room where his father was watching TV.

"Took you long enough to get back here. Where have you been?" Pop asked, completely unaware that Lukas was no longer a teenager living under his roof, as if that mattered.

"I went to have a drink with a couple of the guys I used to work with," Lukas responded with forced casualness.

"So, what's wrong with you?" Pop fixed Lukas a pointed stare.

Lukas cringed. He hated that his father could read him so easily. But he was in no mood to rehash the evening with the man. "Nothing. What do you want for dinner?" Lukas headed for the kitchen and opened the refrigerator. He had only a moment's notice before the door was snatched out of his hand and slammed shut. "Damn, Pop!"

"Don't you stand here and lie to me. Now, what happened?" The old man was at least four inches shorter than his son, but in no way did that diminish the older man's authority. He looked ready to bash Lukas's head in if he didn't start talking, and soon.

Lukas needed to take a deep breath and then rubbed his eyes before he was able to speak. "I ran into Emmy at the bar. She was with Zavia and Isabel."

"And?"

Lukas recounted the entire exchange between him and Emmalyn, or the lack thereof. Just saying the words out loud gave him a pain in his chest that burned like swallowed fire. The heat radiated from his chest to his gut until he thought he was going to be sick. Pop just stood there looking at him like he was the world's biggest idiot.

He told himself that he really only wanted to make sure she was all right, but he recognized the lie. He wanted more, so much more than that. He sighed and leaned heavily against the refrigerator.

"Lukas, you're getting married in a month. It's no business of yours if she is okay or not. Stay away from her."

"Pop, I just wanted to make sure the woman was okay. That's all." The lie tasted salty in his mouth.

"So, why are you all knotted up?" Pop asked. He wanted to reach out and slap his son across the head.

"I don't know." Another salty lie. He needed to get away before his blood pressure went up.

"She left you and broke your heart."

"That's not what happened, and you know it." Lukas tried to push past his father and go up to his room. Stronger than he looked, Pop pushed him back against the refrigerator.

"What I understand better than you is that you have finally gotten over that girl and moved on with your life. You never should have dated her. She always thought she was better than us."

"No, she didn't. She thought she was better than you, and that's because you were so mean to her."

"I was never mean to that girl," Pop defended.

"Her name is Emmy, Pop, not "that girl." And it's a moot point. She doesn't want to talk to me, and she doesn't live in the same place as she did before I moved, so I can't find her. I'm going to bed. Good night."

"Son. Hold up a sec. How do you know she doesn't live in the same place as she did before?" Lukas didn't turn around, but he was pretty sure his father was staring a hole in the back of his head.

"I told you. I wanted to make sure she was okay. You don't have to worry. I'm not going to go looking for her again." Lukas successfully made his escape before his father could respond.

LUKAS LAY IN BED tossing and turning. After a while, he gave up and went down to the kitchen for something to eat. He hadn't eaten at the bar, and after arguing with his father, he never did get around to having dinner. He found his father sitting at the table in the kitchen.

"Pop! What are you doing up? It's after one." Lukas pulled out the chair across from his father. He reached over to the counter behind him and grabbed an apple, wiping it on his shirt before taking a big bite.

"I'm old, and I don't sleep too much these days. Everything hurts, and what doesn't hurt has stopped working. What are you doing up?"

"I was hungry and figured I'd come down and grab a snack to calm my stomach." He took a big bite of the apple then set it down on the table.

"Boy, we have lived in this house all your life. You should remember that your room is directly over this kitchen," said Pop laughing.

"So. What's your point?" Lukas asked the question, but he already knew the answer.

"My point is that your bed has been over my head for the last hour and a half. I've heard you tossing and turning. What's on your mind? Better be your wedding and not Emmalyn Chase."

Lukas had never heard his father call Em by her full name. He was surprised he remembered it after all this time.

"Actually, I was thinking about the wedding," Lukas admitted.

"And Emmalyn," Pop prodded.

"Yes. My brain and my body's reaction to seeing her today has me confused. I honestly thought I was over her. Now? I don't know what to think."

"Do you love Sunny? In your heart of hearts, do you love Sunny?"

"I thought so. But what I feel for Sunny is nothing compared to what I feel for Emmy, even after all this time. I miss Emmy so much, Pop. I miss holding her. I miss kissing her. Hell, I even miss the way she used to dance around the kitchen to annoying teen pop music when she cleaned."

Pop remained silent, lost in his own thoughts. He had never thought Emmalyn was right for his son, and still didn't. But he wanted his son to be happy with the woman waiting for him in California, not with the witch that had broken him years before. "So, why are you marrying Sunny?" he finally asked.

"Honestly? Because I want a family. I'm ready to settle down. I didn't think I'd ever have a second chance with Emmalyn, and I knew I needed to stop waiting for her. Sunny is a great woman—kind, compassionate, caring." His voice trailed off, and he tried to picture his fiancée in his mind. The only image he could muster was Emmalyn. That couldn't be a good sign.

"That's not a reason to marry a woman, Lukas. I taught you better than that. I married your mother because she was always the only woman in the room. I could never see anyone else but her, no matter who else was around. You're using one woman as a replacement for another woman and that just isn't fair, to any of you."

"So, what are you saying? I should call off my engagement to Sunny? And tell her what? Then I'll have two women that hate my guts." Lukas tossed the apple core into the trash, got out of the chair and got a glass of water. He thought about what his father was saying. Was Sunny just a replacement for Emmy?

"I'm saying that perhaps you need to close the chapter with Emmalyn before you open a new one with Sunny."

"And how should I do that? She doesn't want to see me, and I've been warned off by her friends. I don't want to make things worse with her." Lukas's voice was just a hair shy of whining. He groaned.

Pop laughed, a full belly laugh, at his son's expense. "Do you really think you are going to make things worse? She's running from you in bars. That's pretty bad, son."

Lukas chuckled at his father's logic. He kissed the top of his father's head as he walked back toward the stairs. "Thanks, Pop. I needed this chat."

Pop hesitated before calling out, "If you really want to see her, she works downtown at Carlson Design Consultants. Be very sure of what you want before you go after her. And remember the woman waiting to marry you back west." Pop laughed at himself. His son had turned out to be more like him than he'd thought. "Quite the mess you've created for yourself, my boy. Quite the mess indeed."

Lukas climbed the staircase, went to his room, and got back into bed. He continued to toss and turn, but this time it was excitement keeping him awake. He'd finally come up with a fool-proof plan to convince his Emmy to talk to him

5 ONE THING OR ANOTHER

"OH, MY GOD, ISABEL, will you please go home? I'm fine. And I know you have better things to do today—like work. Please. Go." Emmalyn hated the begging tone her voice had taken on, but three days of Isabel and Zavia babysitting her was driving her insane.

"It's no problem. I don't mind keeping you company." Isabel and Em had been friends long enough for Isabel to know that Em wasn't talking about taking advantage of her time. Em wasn't fine. Any idiot could see. And as anxious as Isabel was to get back to her own life—she'd had to cancel two dates already—she didn't want to leave her friend to fall into darkness alone.

"You know damned well that is not what I meant! I don't want to have to do this, but I'm throwing you out of my house. Get out!"

Said with a smile and a knowing look, Isabel didn't take offense. In truth, she really was ready to go home.

"Fine. But I'm calling Zavia and telling her to check on you later today." Isabel jumped off the bed in the guest room and began stuffing her clothes in her bag. Em stood in the doorway watching, amused by how little Isabel cared about the clothes that had been strewn around the room. She was the exact opposite of Zavia.

"I love you both. I really do. Since Mom moved away with her new husband, I've been so afraid I'd be all alone here. But, somehow, I seem to always have someone bossing me around."

Isabel paused. "We don't boss you around, exactly. We just make sure you don't make a disaster of your life." Isabel dropped to the floor in search of her other shoe. Em spotted the bright orange sneaker first and walked over and picked the shoe up. She held it out to her friend but stopped just out of Isabel's reach.

"That is totally the same thing," Em pointed out with a slight grin.

Isabel lunged forward and snatched the shoe out of Em's hand. "Not even—bossing you around just makes it sound like we want you to do what we say. Helping you not to make a disaster of your life is just that— helping. See the difference?" Isabel couldn't stop the giggles from escaping. Em's frown was as expected as the sunrise.

"No, not really." Em stood aside as Isabel stalked out the room. She took another look at the room her friend had been staying in for just a weekend. The small space was utter chaos. She exhaled a deep sigh and turned down the stairs to the kitchen where Isabel was preparing coffee in one of Em's favorite travel mugs.

Em sauntered to the cabinet and grabbed a different travel mug for Isabel to take and then lose. She snatched the carafe of fresh coffee out of Isabel's hand and poured the liquid in before handing the mug back to Isabel.

"Hey, I like the other cup better."

"So do I, which is why you're taking this one. I won't have to track you down and kill you to get my mug back." Em gave her a wide smile. "You're going to be late for work if you don't get out of here."

"I'm glad you're taking the day off. You need to rest your brain. It's been a shitty few days."

"Yeah, well, we'll see how happy you are when you get to the office and all hell has broken loose."

Isabel snatched up her tote bag and her purse and headed for the door. She stopped with her hand on the knob and spoke to Em over her shoulder.

"I understand you still love him, but I really hope you can see that this situation can't work. You do see that—don't you?"

"What if he has changed?" Em asked that more to herself than to Isabel, but she wasn't fool enough to think Isabel wouldn't answer.

"Even if he has changed, will that solve everything?" Isabel turned and faced Em full on. "Suppose he's changed and is everything you ever wanted of him. Would you be able to trust him not to hurt you again? Can you live with constantly waiting for the other shoe to drop? Is that really the life you want?

"Zavia thinks you should stay as far away from him as you can. I can see why she'd say that, but I disagree. I think you need to face him and know that you are making the right choice no matter what. You aren't the same person you were five years ago. Your dad dying affected you in ways you could never have guessed, and you put everything— your love and your grief—into your relationship with Lukas, rightly or wrongly. He couldn't be what you needed then, and I don't think he can be what you need now." Isabel dropped her bags and rushed over to pull Em into yet another tight embrace.

"I know how much you hate hugs, but I needed this one," Isabel admitted.

Em sighed and let her body relax into the hug. "It's okay. I think I needed this one too."

"Okay, enough of that. I'm off. If you need anything, please, please, please don't hesitate to call. Zavia isn't teaching today and she has only a few client meetings, so she can come too."

"Okay. I will. Now go before I get us both in trouble with Meanie Martin." At the sound of their private nickname for their boss, Isabel's eyes went wide, and she ran out of the house and jumped in her car. Em watched from the doorway as Isabel flew down the driveway and down the street.

"That girl is going to kill someone one day." Em shook her head and went back into the house.

As she headed back to clean the spare room, she began to think about what Isabel had said. Should she face Lukas? Could she? Was she really strong enough for that? She honestly didn't know. Spying on him in a bar while drunk was one thing. Actually talking to him was another. What Em did know was that she wasn't ready at that moment for any kind of confrontation. And with that thought in mind, she resolved herself to staying as far away from Lukas Upton as humanly possible.

ISABEL KNEW AS SOON as she walked in the door that Em was right. All hell had broken loose in the office. She tried to get to the small office she and Em shared as quietly as possible, but that plan was quickly derailed as the office manager spied her less than five feet from her door.

"Isabel! Oh, thank heavens you're here. We've got a new client waiting, and Emmalyn waited until this morning to let us know she wasn't coming in today." Barbara drew out Emmalyn's name dramatically, causing Isabel to roll her eyes. She ducked into her office with Barbara hot on her heels. She took a moment to set her coffee down and fall heavily into her desk chair. Taking an extra deep breath before turning to face Barbara, she plastered on a wide but insincere smile.

"Okay. Tell me what's going. Slowly." Isabel took a long sip of her coffee, savoring the strong flavor. Emmalyn's deeply ingrained caffeine addiction was starting to rub off on her, she thought, blocking out the sounds of Barbara's high-pitched chattering.

Barbara huffed, her ample bosom straining against the clearly-too-small, white oxford blouse she wore. "We have a new client waiting in the conference room. They asked to meet with you and Emmalyn. I let the client know that Emmalyn would not be in the office today, and they said they would wait to meet with you."

"See, that wasn't so hard. Now let's go see what this new client needs."

Isabel grabbed a notepad and pen and walked out of her office. She got halfway to the door and remembered to grab her coffee off the desk. She walked down the hall to the conference room, pausing at the door to take a sip of her coffee before entering the room. There were three gentlemen sitting around the oval conference table, two of whom she already knew. As her eyes rested on Lukas, she spit out her coffee, getting the scalding-hot liquid all over her fairly new, butter-yellow silk blouse and across the floor. Lukas smiled serenely at Isabel as he stood up to offer her a handkerchief.

"What the hell are you doing here?" Isabel stared at Lukas in pure disbelief. He held on to his smile at her but was smart enough not to respond. Isabel tried to speak again, but her boss walked into the conference room with a disapproving look on his face.

"Isabel. Is there a problem?" he asked, his voice full of false sincerity and condescension.

Isabel tried to pull herself together as she turned to face Meanie Martin.

"No, sir. Can you excuse us for a moment? Please, just one second." Isabel reached out and grabbed Lukas by the hand. She pulled him out of the chair and dragged him down the narrow hallway to her office. She shoved the much larger man in the room and closed the door behind her.

"Lukas Upton, I swear to God. You have got to be kidding me. What in the name of all things holy are you doing here? Emmalyn can't find you here." Isabel began pacing her office, trying to decide whether to call Zavia or just kill Lukas where he stood. The placid look on his face did nothing to soothe her nerves.

"I need to see her, Isabel. You have to understand," pleaded Lukas quietly.

"No! What I understand is that you need to stay away from her, unless and until she comes to talk to you."

"Why are you and Zavia trying so hard to protect her? She's not as fragile as you guys think."

"How the fuck would you know? Listen, Lukas. I'm going to level with you. She fell apart after the two of you broke up. It took months for her to get back on her feet and so many months more before she got back to normal. She doesn't need you messing with her mind again, trying to convince her that you love her when the whole time the only person you care about is yourself."

"That is not how things went down, and you know it. And in case you forgot, she threw me out!" he whispered furiously.

A knock on the door interrupted the conversation. Isabel opened the door and asked Barbara for just a few more minutes. She closed the door and leaned her head against the thin wood, taking a moment to get her thoughts together before speaking.

"Did Em ever tell you about her dad? About what he was like?" Isabel was well aware she was treading on very thin ice with this topic, but she needed Lukas to understand.

"No. I would ask her, but she would never say anything. I know he died, and it broke her heart."

Isabel smiled at the memories swirling in her mind. "Her dad was amazing, one of the best men I ever met—when he was sober. But he was very, very rarely sober. And he spent her whole life making promises to her to get better, to get help, to finally get sober. He would make plans to do things with her and never show because he'd get drunk. He missed every important milestone in her life." Isabel paused and stood up straight. She turned and moved to stand directly in front of Lukas. She stared directly into his eyes as she spoke.

"The day he died, he should have been with Em and her mom, but he didn't show, didn't come home. They were broken because they knew something had happened. The phone call they'd always known was coming finally came the next morning."

"Isabel, I swear I didn't know." Lukas felt like the heel of a shoe that just stepped in dog poop.

Isabel pressed on. "And now, you do. I mean, didn't it seem odd that she would put such importance on promises? Not honesty or fidelity or any of the other things most women care about? Damn it, Lukas, you could have beaten her every day, and she would have stayed with you forever. She asked one thing of you, and you couldn't give that one thing to her. I am begging you. Whatever you think you need to say to her, please don't. Just stay away from her." Isabel walked out of the office, leaving Lukas to consider her words.

A Free Lunch

ACCORDING TO PSYCHOLOGY, THERE are five love languages. The trick to winning at love is to find someone whose language is compatible with yours. If you need someone to tell you he or she loves you, then you need to find someone who can do that. If you need to be shown love, because hearing it isn't enough, then that's the kind of person you need to be with.

Lukas learned enough in his sole psychology class to recognize that he and Emmalyn loved and needed love in completely different ways. Lukas was loud and proud with his feelings for Em. Everyone he met knew exactly how he felt about her.

Emmalyn, on the other hand, was quiet and strong. In her experience, she knew that words were often useless. She needed someone who could express their love by being exactly what they promised to be. And though they loved each other intensely, their inability to love the same doomed their relationship.

Lukas had been thinking about this for some time. He knew Em still loved him and he had finally accepted that he was still very much in love with her. Every time he saw her, his resolve to make things right with her strengthened. But he couldn't get the conversation with Isabel out of his mind. Lukas knew that there had been issues between Em and her dad, but Isabel was right — he had never asked her what happened.

Unable to fall asleep for the second night in a row, Lukas went down to the kitchen for something to drink and found his father sitting at the table eating cookies.

"Seriously, Pop, it's two o'clock in the morning. What are you doing up and eating cookies?"

"As I told you last night when you asked that same damn question, I'm old. What are you doing up again tonight?"

Lukas sat down across from his father and watched him. His father cocked an eyebrow at him askance.

"I need to talk to someone, and I need you to try not to be judgmental or intolerant."

His father threw his head back and laughed. "Then why talk to me?"

"Cuz you're the only one here." The two laughed quietly, lost in thought.

"So, what have you done now?" asked Pop, clearly amused.

"I went to Em's office to talk to her. And before you say anything, she wasn't there. I talked to Isabel, trying to get her to tell me what's up with Em. She told me about Em's dad and why she is so obsessed with promises and keeping my word. I honestly didn't know it was so important to her. I never tried to hurt her; I just figured she always had her friends with her, and it didn't matter if I was there or not. That, apparently, was not the case."

"So, what, exactly, is your plan? You can't go chasing after one woman while you are engaged to another. That isn't fair to either of them."

"I know. I wanted to get things straight with Em so I could marry Sunny."

Pop thought about that statement for a moment before asking, "Do you want to know if there is some hope of getting back with Emmalyn or to be sure it's over?"

"I don't know. I just think — I don't know what to think anymore."

Lukas stood up from the table and headed for the stairs. His foot had hit the first stair when he heard his father's voice. "Can I make a suggestion without sounding judgmental or intolerant?"

"Probably not," Lukas admitted, "but give it a try."

"I suggest you stay away from Emmalyn and Sunny until you know the answer to that question."

Lukas gave the idea some thought. "You may be right with that one. Thanks, Pop."

AFTER TEN EXCRUCIATING MINUTES of staring at a blank screen, Emmalyn, or more correctly her stomach, realized she was absolutely starving. She looked around her office to find that Isabel was still in her design meeting. She quickly grabbed her purse and headed down to the little Irish pub on the ground floor of her office building to get something to eat in peace and quiet.

For the past week, Isabel and Zavia had been all over her, trying to make sure she was all right. Nothing she said seemed to convince her two best friends that she really did feel better about life and Lukas. She understood that they meant well and that their concern was justified, but so much togetherness was driving Em insane.

Happy to be able to eat in silence for once, Em took a seat at the far end of the bar away from the window — just in case Zavia or Isabel came looking for her. She considered ordering the fish and chips, but, in the end, she opted for a burger and fries. Taking her sweet time to people watch and silently judge, Emmalyn took a big bite of her burger and nearly choked when her most recent ex, Grant, walked in. Clearly unable to crawl under the bar and hide, she smiled at him, then quickly remembered the mouth full of meat that required chewing and swallowing. She covered her mouth, finished chewing, and took a big swallow of soda as Grant took the stool next to her.

"Hi. I'm surprised to see you here." Grant reached down and grabbed a french fry off Em's plate, then quickly put it back. "Sorry about that. I remember how much you hate that."

His smile threw Em off a bit. Grant was very handsome, with golden-brown skin, a full beard, and a freshly shaven baldhead. Em often wondered why he wanted to be with her, when it was obvious he could be with any woman he wanted.

"I work upstairs in this building, remember. I don't eat here often, but I took a few minutes to grab something quick to eat." She wiped her mouth before swiveling around on the stool the give the man beside her, her full attention.

"Well, don't let me interrupt your meal. I was passing by and saw you from the street. I just wanted to say hello." Grant popped a French fry in his mouth and stood up. He turned to walk away then hesitated. Unfortunately, he turned back to Em in time to see her take another big bite of burger. Em inelegantly spit the burger on her plate and wiped her mouth. Grant didn't have the heart to tell her that she had lettuce in her teeth. Instead, he laughed quietly, then asked her, "Are you free for dinner tonight?"

"Gee, I don't know," Em hemmed and hawed, looking for a way to get out of this conversation. Her mind conveniently went blank, making her sound like a broken record.

Grant sat back down on the stool next to Em. "Emmalyn, look, I really like you. I'm just asking for dinner. I'm sure there is a very good reason for why you keep running away from me. Think about it, and give me a call. I'd really like to see you."

He stood up and walked away before Em could answer. She signaled the bartender with her hand and asked for a box for her burger and fries. She hastily paid for her food and hurried back to her office. Em was so deep in thought as she stepped off the elevator that she walked smack into Isabel.

"Where in the hell have you been? I've been looking all over for you," Isabel exclaimed.

Isabel grabbed Em's arm and pulled her down the hall into their shared office. She slammed the door shut as Em flopped down into her chair and opened the box containing her now cold lunch.

"Well! What have you got to say for yourself?" demanded Isabel.

"I got hungry," Em offered to a clearly unamused Isabel a cold french fry. Em sighed, dropped the fry back into the box, and slumped down into her chair. "I noticed that you and Zavia had finally crawled out of my ass, and I went — all by my lonesome – to get something to eat. Is that a crime?"

"We've been worried about you. And speaking of worrywarts, Lukas has been here looking for you."

"Well, damn. It's truly raining men! I ran into Grant in the bar downstairs," Em replied with a dramatic toss of her hands.

"What did he want?" Isabel asked.

"What did Lukas want?" Em retorted.

Isabel moved to the chair across from Em and began eating her fries. "He wanted to tell you he was going back to California. Your turn."

"Grant wants to go to dinner tonight," Em conceded.

"Are you going to go?"

"Is Lukas really leaving town?"

"Yes. He wanted to say good-bye. I think you should go—to dinner, that is."

Finishing off the fries, Isabel hopped up and went back to sit at her desk. There was a quick knock on the door before Zavia walked in, carrying food.

"Hiya, ladies. What's going on?"

Isabel jumped up and closed the door. "Lemme catch you up. Lukas is heading back to California, and Grant asked Em to dinner tonight. So, Em, what're you going to do?"

Em looked up at her two best friends. How could she tell them that she didn't want to go out with Grant; she wanted to go after Lukas? She knew full well she couldn't do that and have them ever leave her alone again. Besides, he was leaving town. She heaved a deep sigh and said, "I'm going to go to dinner with Grant tonight. He says it's just dinner. What harm can it do?"

7 Dinner & Drama

EMMALYN MET GRANT LATER that evening at a
fairly swanky seafood restaurant on the riverfront.
They ordered wine and an appetizer, making small talk
while waiting for their food. Em couldn't help but notice how good Grant looked in his suit. He embodied
all the qualities she'd ever wanted in a man. In fact, he
was the most reliable man she knew and always followed through on all his promises. Grant was everything Lukas wasn't. But still — there was something
missing. She couldn't identify why, but she didn't love
Grant, not the way she loved Lukas.

Em understood that she needed to get over and
past Lukas. He, obviously, was no good for her, but she
didn't know how to get him out of her system. On the

cab ride to the restaurant, she had decided to give Grant a chance. He deserved that much from her. She was completely absorbed in her thoughts when she noticed that Grant was talking to her.

"Hello... anyone home?" Grant asked, cutting in on her thoughts.

Emmalyn smiled and apologized. "I was lost in thought there for a minute."

"Whatcha thinking of, if I may ask?"

"Of course you can. I was thinking of you. And me. And us—if I'm going to be completely honest."

"And what did you conclude?" Grant leaned back in his chair and studied Em, causing her to squirm in her chair.

"I haven't concluded yet. But I'm open to discussion and the presentation of additional data." Emmalyn laughed at herself and took a sip of her wine.

"Emmalyn, I want to be completely honest with you. I really want to give our relationship another chance. I've missed you, and I want to be with you again."

"Grant, I..." Luckily for Em the conversation was interrupted by the arrival of their entrees. She had no idea what to say to that candid confession. She was pretty sure that she had little feeling for him beyond friendship. And although she was amenable to resuming dating, she didn't feel good about leading him on. Her brain wasn't working fast enough to figure out an answer that didn't begin and end with the word um.

As the food was being set down, Emmalyn thought frantically about what needed to happen next. Her panic must have been evident on her face. Grant reached across the table and took her hand in his. "I want you to think about what I've said. Don't decide anything right now. I don't want you to say yes because I railroaded you into anything. Let's just enjoy dinner and a nice evening out." He smiled brightly at her and poured more wine into her glass.

"Thank you, Grant. You really are the sweetest man I've ever met."

"And you are the most amazing woman I've ever met. Now! Let's change the subject. Have you been watching much football this season? The Panthers are looking awfully dangerous this year."

Emmalyn laughed heartily at that. "You clearly haven't been paying attention. Watch more SportsCenter."

The rest of the meal went by smoothly. Em and Grant were able to eat, drink, and be generally merry. The conversation flowed easily and both seemed to really enjoy the evening. They split a dessert of chocolate cake and ice cream, and finished off the bottle of wine. All was well with the evening. No further mention of relationships was made, and Em was truly enjoying herself for the first time in a long time.

Em was finishing off her last glass of wine and thinking to herself that she needed to find a way to convince Grant to take things at a slower pace, when she spotted Brian and Lukas being led to a table in the bar area of the restaurant. Em choked on her wine, dropping her glass in her lap. Grant jumped up and tried to help Em mop up the mess she made on her clothes.

Lukas noticed the commotion across the restaurant and spied Emmalyn and her date. He turned to walk over there but was stopped by Brian.

"Man, what do you think you're doing? You can't go over there. She's out on a date with another dude." Brian couldn't believe he even needed to tell Lukas any of this. The man had lost all of his good senses.

"I just want to talk to her. No biggie."

"Huge biggie! Let her be, man. You're heading back home tomorrow—back to your fiancée. Nothing good is going to come from you busting in on her date." Brian simply could not fathom that Lukas was even considering going over there. He shook his head and groaned.

"I don't care. I just need to talk to her."

Lukas jerked his arm away from Brian and rushed over to the table where Em and Grant were sitting.

"Emmalyn, we need to talk," Lukas demanded.

"I don't think so. I'm on a date." Em refused to even make eye contact with Lukas, keeping her eyes on her date.

"Emmy, listen…," he implored, desperate to talk to her. Seeing her here with another man stabbed him in the gut. His mind knew the feeling was ridiculous — he was engaged to another woman for God's sake — but he had to do something, even if that something was making things worse.

"Do. Not. Do that! I'm on a date," she all but growled. She slammed her glass down, but still refused to look at Lukas.

It was clear that Emmalyn was getting upset. Instead of taking the hint and walking away, Lukas sat down at the table. Grant began to interject, but Emmalyn cut him off.

"Grant, you don't have to say anything." She finally turned to look at the man that had been plaguing her mind for some weeks now. The look was not friendly. "Lukas, I have absolutely nothing to say to you. You need to get up and leave this table immediately, or I will get the restaurant to put you out."

He looked as though he was going to argue when Brian stepped in to pull him away.

"Lukas. We need to go. Security is heading this way."

"Fine. Emmalyn, you'll have to talk to me at some point. You can call me anytime." Lukas shot one final look at Grant, then at Emmalyn, then walked away from the table and out of the restaurant.

"I'm so sorry about that Grant. There are a thousand restaurants in this city. Why is he always in the one I'm at? I don't get it."

"Who is he?" Grant asked, instantly understanding exactly why Em had been so reluctant to commit to him.

"An ex-boyfriend. We broke up a long while ago, and he left town. I'd heard he was going back to wherever it was he came from but not soon enough to not jack up my evening, apparently."

"Hmmmm. And was he the reason you choked on your wine?"

Em looked guilty and smiled, her cheeks going red from an intense blush. "Can I plead the fifth? I was surprised to see him here. Like I said, I was under the impression that he'd left town. I'm really sorry."

"It's okay. That actually answers a couple of questions I had." Emmalyn opened her mouth to argue, but Grant stopped her. "You don't have to explain anything. It really is okay. Would you like me to take you home?"

"No, thanks. I think I need some time to work through everything that has happened this evening."

"Do you need me to stay with you?" he asked, equal parts hopeful and concerned.

She smiled as she reached out to cup his face. "You really are the sweetest man. But no, I'll be okay. I took a cab to get here, and I have the guy's number to pick me up when I am ready. I'll be fine. I swear. How about I call you tomorrow, and we can go to dinner again, my treat?"

He took her hand and kissed her fingertips. "If you're absolutely sure. And I'd love to go to dinner again." Grant leaned down and kissed Emmalyn softly on the lips. "Despite the madness, I had fun tonight.

I'll talk to you later." He kissed her again on the forehead and walked out of the restaurant.

EMMALYN WATCHED GRANT WALK outside be-
fore heading over to the bar. She sat on a stool away
from the other patrons, ordered a glass of chardonnay,
and began to think. Her evening with Grant was going
wonderfully until Lukas showed up. She'd almost convinced herself that renewing a relationship with Grant
would be a good thing. But seeing Lukas made her
stomach flip and her heart race in a way that Grant
never had. So what to do now? Lukas was supposed to
be heading back to California. What the hell was he
still doing here? Em's mind raced. Grant was here and
available, and he wanted to be with her. After three
glasses of wine, Emmalyn was more confused than ever. She finally gave up trying to find answers in a wine
bottle and decided to go home.

She walked out of the restaurant, looking for her
phone to call the cabbie to take her back to her house.
The cool air felt good on her face. She closed her eyes
and took in a deep breath of the nighttime air. She
didn't realize she was being watched until she heard
Lukas's voice.

"Jeez, Emmalyn. I was about ready to go in after
you."

Startled, Em jumped and dropped her phone. She turned to Lukas, angry and embarrassed. "Oh, good grief, Lukas. I thought you were going away. What in the hell are you still doing here?"

Lukas walked over to her and picked up her phone from where it lay on the sidewalk. For several seconds, he said nothing, causing Em to fidget. "Emmalyn, I'm going back to California tomorrow. Can we please talk?"

"About what, exactly," she sighed warily. She recognized this for the bad idea it was.

"About us."

"There is no us. There hasn't been an 'us' for a while now. And for the record, interrupting my date is not the least bit endearing."

"I'm very sorry about that, but I've been trying to get you to talk to me for weeks now. Please. Just ten minutes. I'll drive you home, say what I need to say, and be out of your life."

She rolled her eyes and gave up trying to run away. "Fine. Let's roll. My buzz is wearing off."

8 HITTING REPLAY

THE RIDE STARTED OFF in silence. Emmalyn was immediately aware that taking a ride from Lukas would not end well, but short of jumping out of the moving vehicle, she was stuck. She'd finally decided to get to the bottom of this "talk" when he turned to her and asked her if she still loved him.

"What? What kind of question is that?" she insisted. The wine and his insane question were on the verge of giving Em a splitting headache.

"I need to know. Emmalyn, please. Do you still love me?"

Emmalyn gave Lukas a loud and inelegant snort. "I am not having this conversation with you."

"Emmy, listen..." He wanted to explain everything to her, but before he could get his thoughts in order, she cut him off.

"No! I am not talking about this with you. It took me a long time to get on with my life after we broke up. I'm not going down that road with you. Period."

Lukas knew from the look on her face that pushing the issue wouldn't help anything. He left her to her own thoughts as he continued driving toward her house. She even seem annoyed at having to give him directions — as if he should know where she lived now! He couldn't help but wonder why she would have a hard time moving on when she was the one who broke things off with him. After his chat with Isabel, Lukas thought he understood a bit better how Em's mind worked. Perhaps he could have approached the conversation differently, but she used to appreciate his straight forward questions.

They arrived at Em's house before either of them could find something else to say. He was impressed by her new home and even more so by the woman she'd become in the years they'd been apart. They sat in the driveway in silence, neither knowing what to say to the other. Finally, tired of the tension and needing something—not quite sure what—Em turned and looked at Lukas.

"Just come in the house." She quickly got out of the car before she could change her mind about what she was about to do.

Lukas followed Em into the house, clearly confused. He trailed her from room to room as she turned on lights and fed the pretty gray cat that swirled around her legs. He watched the ease with which she stooped and swept up the cat in a bit of a snuggle. His thoughts turned sour as he found himself in the ridiculous position of being insanely jealous of a house cat.

She stopped in the kitchen and pulled a bottle of water out of the refrigerator. She offered him one and shrugged her shoulders when he declined. Emmalyn took a long sip of water before turning to Lukas. He couldn't read the look on her face and was taken completely by surprise by what she said.

"I want to have sex with you. Tonight." She took another drink of water and waited for him to process what she'd said to him.

Lukas couldn't tell if she was serious or not, so he said nothing. She gave him a small smile and said, "I'm serious. We both know you and I are done. But I want tonight, no talking, no thinking. Tomorrow you go back to California and I go back to Grant."

"Emmalyn, that's crazy." He shook his head and turned to leave the house.

"Is there someone else?" she asked quietly, suddenly very unsure of herself.

Lukas paused at the kitchen door. He knew he should tell her the truth, tell her about his life with Sunny. But she was offering what his body and, if he were completely honest with himself, his heart had been yearning for ever since he'd seen her his first night back in town. Hating himself for what he was doing, yet unable to stop himself, he turned back to her fully before simply saying, "No."

"Then what's so crazy? I'm not asking for anything we haven't done before, unless you've learned something new in the time we've been apart," she added saucily.

That got the expected smile from Lukas. He reached out and stroked her cheek and chin. "Are you sure you want to do this? I don't want to make things any worse between us than they already are. And I don't want to make any more waves between you and your little boyfriend."

"I'm a big girl, and I can make my own decisions, thanks very much."

Emmalyn leaned forward and kissed Lukas softly yet thoroughly on the lips. She slowly slid her hands up his face and wrapped her arms around his neck. Lukas responded to the kiss by wrapping his arms around Em's waist and pulling her close. He deepened the kiss, slowly sliding his tongue into her mouth. The kiss brought back every warm feeling and happy memory that Emmalyn worked so hard to suppress over the last five years. She pulled back from him but remained in Lukas's arms.

"Second thoughts?" he asked, his voice gruff from the strain of fighting the urge to toss her onto the nearest surface and pour himself into her.

Lukas had a half smile on his face and seemed prepared for Em to tell him to go.

"Nope. Let's go to the bedroom."

Em took Lukas's hand and led him up the stairs to the third level of her house. The master bedroom sat at the end of a long hallway. Once there, she turned on a single lamp, throwing deep shadows across the ornate, cherry oak furniture. As if in her dreams, Em and Lukas stood next to the bed unsure how to start. Finally, Emmalyn reached over and began unbuttoning Lukas's shirt. He swatted her hands away and pulled her close once again, claiming her lips in a kiss that left her nearly breathless. He pulled her blouse out of her skirt and over her head, tossing it on the floor. He felt her breasts through the fabric of her bra, the tight buds of her nipples poking through, hinting at her arousal. Pushing the straps off her shoulders, he trailed kisses where the straps left light marks, his mouth so warm against her skin. Reaching behind her with one hand to unhook her bra, he pulled her over to the bed, sitting on the edge.

Positioning Em between his legs, his dark and wild eyes devoured her as he played with her breasts before pulling one nipple then the other into his mouth—he remembered how much she liked that. When she couldn't stand it anymore, she pulled away from him and took a step back, removing her skirt and panties in a single yank. His mouth watered as she sauntered back to him, pushed him back on the bed, climbed on top of him, kissed him hard. He scooted back on the bed, taking her with him before flipping her over on her back.

He reached down and removed his own pants and underwear before quickly filling her. He felt like an ass for not at least checking to see if she was wet, but her moans of pleasure and sounds of reassurance quickly buried those thoughts.

She met him stroke for stroke, his member hitting that special spot that only he had ever been able to find. As the tension built in her gut, she grabbed on to his butt for dear life, like she was afraid the buck on top of her would get away. It wasn't long before the sweet, taut pressure built to release, and she came, crying out his name in satisfaction. He let himself go soon thereafter, wholly unable to withstand the pressure any longer. In the pleasure of it all, he collapsed on top of her. They fell asleep that way—her legs wrapped around his waist, her arms around his neck, and her hair wrapped around his hand.

9 ONE BITTER PILL

THE NIGHT WAS LONG and pleasurable. Lukas finally peeled himself away from his sweet Emmy and out of her bed around dawn. She didn't stir. He kissed her nose and left before any regrets or harsh words could pass between them.

But no matter how relaxed and at peace he was with what had happened between them, Lukas couldn't help but dread the coming conversation with his father about his overnight absence. He'd never been able to lie to his father, no matter how big or small the lie. Somehow his father always knew when he was being untruthful, and he was very sure a fight was about to ensue.

Pulling up to the house, Lukas took a deep breath and steeled himself for battle. It hit him as soon as he walked in the front door.

"Where the hell have you been? I called your cell phone so many times and left so many messages. How could you let me worry about you like this? So childish and irresponsible! Well, what have you got to say for yourself?" Pop was pacing furiously in the house's small foyer.

"If I could get a word in edgewise, I'd tell you what happened, but I'd really like a cup of coffee before we start today's inquisition." Lukas brushed past his father and headed toward the kitchen.

"Were you with Emmalyn? You were, weren't you?" He followed Lukas down the hall, close on his heels.

"Pop, can we please not do this? I'm a grown man. Where I was and what I was doing are none of your business. So let's skip this."

"And your fiancée? What do you think she will think about you spending the night with some snotty bitch you used to hook up with five years ago?"

"Are you threatening me old man?" Lukas asked menacingly. He didn't believe for a moment his father was going to call Sunny, but making threats to produce guilt—yes, that was his specialty.

"Tell me where you were," Pop demanded.

Lukas sighed and gave his father what he'd wanted. "Fine. I was with Emmalyn. I went to talk to her, and things went too far. I can't say I'm sorry it happened though."

"I didn't raise you to be a liar and cheater," Pop growled.

"This is no big deal, pop. It's out of my system and I'll get over her. I've done it before."

"So, she's turned her back on you again, huh? I told you she was nothing but trouble for you. I don't know why you get drawn to that tramp. Over and over she proves to be too high and mighty for you, but you can't seem to help yourself." Pop couldn't seem to stop himself from fussing at his oldest son. But he had to make the boy understand that women like Emmalyn Chase weren't for him.

"You want to know why I keep getting drawn back to her? Because I love her! I have loved her from the moment I first saw her, and I will love her until I die."

"So where does that leave me?" came a soft, feminine voice from the direction of the stairwell.

Lukas instantly recognized the voice, and his head dropped to the table. He struggled between going to comfort Sunny and murdering his father in his own kitchen.

"You are a meddlesome old man who will die alone," Lukas growled at his father as he walked over to Sunny.

"It leaves you the same as ever," he said to her softly and, he hoped, reassuringly, "the woman I'm planning to marry in three months. I hope one mistake doesn't change that. It doesn't for me, at least."

Sunny looked at Lukas, then at Pop. Tears welling in her eyes, head shaking in disbelief, she turned and ran back upstairs without saying a word in response.

"How you gonna marry that girl and be vowing to love someone else until you die?" Lukas's father asked with a skeptical laugh.

"I swear to God, old man, stay out of this. This is all your fault! I lost Emmy because of you, and if I lose Sunny, it will be your fault as well." He racked his brain for something to say to Sunny that would fix this mess. "When did you call her?" Lukas demanded.

"Two days ago," he replied proudly. "You needed to see what you're doing, acting as you have been. Sunny is a good woman, and she is perfect for you. Emmalyn and you don't belong together. You never did," Pop asserted self-righteously.

"How the hell would you know that?" Lukas yelled at his father. " You've barely said ten words to her. And how do you know about Sunny? You've never met her before today."

Pop gasped. "I could tell over the phone that she was better for you than that Emmalyn."

Lukas angrily shook his head. "This is ridiculous. I'm not having this conversation with you. I need to talk to Sunny."

Lukas stood up and headed for the stairs. He stopped abruptly when he realized his father was following closely behind him. He turned on the man angrily. "Where in the hell do you think you're going?"

"To make sure you don't ruin things with that girl!" Pop knew in his rickety bones that Lukas needed to make things right with Sunny to be happy.

"Oh my God! Stay here." Lukas ran up the stairs and walked into the only room with a closed door on the second floor of his childhood home. "Grab a sweater. We're going out," Lukas said to Sunny.

"What? Lukas, we need to talk, I think."

"I wholeheartedly agree." He reached into her bag and grabbed the first thing that looked like a sweater and tossed it to her. He then grabbed her purse and pulled her off the bed and through the door. "We can talk someplace where we can be alone."

They stumbled down the stairs toward the front door. "Lukas, are you sure about this?"

"I've never been more sure about anything in my life." Lukas stopped at the door and turned to his father. "Stay out of this, and stay out of my way. I will never forgive you for this if I live to be a hundred."

"I'm only trying to keep you from making a huge mistake." His answer was made to the slamming door.

THE TENSION IN THE car was thick as Lukas and Sunny drove away from his father's house. It was clear that he wanted to say something but wasn't sure how to start. He opened and closed his mouth five times before Sunny, unable to wait any longer, spoke first.

"Lukas. You have to say something, please," she exclaimed.

"I still want to marry you," he announced, certain he was making the wrong decision but equally certain there was no other choice for him.

"That may not be possible." She paused, her face thoughtful. "Tell me about her. Did you sleep with her? And why have you never mentioned her before?" Sunny was honestly confused that Lukas had never before mentioned someone who was still so clearly important to him.

"What else don't I know about him?" she thought to herself.

"I never mentioned her because it's always too hard to talk about Emmalyn. I fell in love with her long ago. She was a student back when I worked in the computer lab at the university. It was instant and deep."

"So what happened? Why aren't you two together then? Why aren't you with her now," Sunny asked, though she was afraid that no matter what the answer, it would mean the end of their relationship.

"I always put everyone and everything ahead of her. And when she really needed me, I wasn't there, so she broke things off with me. I hadn't seen or spoken to her in over five years, until I ran into her here," Lukas confessed sadly.

"And how could you sleep with her and then tell me you still want to marry me? I heard your grand declaration of love for her Lukas, and I can tell you, you have never said anything like that about me or to me. I don't think you feel anything for me like what you claim you felt and, clearly, still feel about her. Why should we move forward with anything when you, evidently, would rather be with her?" Sunny had begun to cry again. Lukas felt lower than ever.

"The plain truth is that I don't have a future with Emmalyn. I have one with you. No matter what I feel for her, she and I are done. Last night was a purging of a kind. She and I agreed to one night, with no further conversation, no talk of the future, just a way to get each other out of our systems."

Lukas parked the car near the riverwalk. He and Sunny sat and watched the water for a while before anyone could speak.

"Is she? Is she out of your system? Do you love me the way you love Emmalyn?"

"She's over for me. I can't speak for her, but I... I know the end when I see it and I really wish I hadn't run into her. She was better off in my past. I promise you that." Lukas hoped he sounded sincere, because even as the words were coming out of his mouth, he knew he was lying. "I will completely understand if you want to end our relationship because of what I did. It's no more than what I deserve for betraying your trust like that.

"To be honest, I don't know if I can live with what you did, but I'm not ready to call it quits just yet. I don't know anything right now except that I want to go back to San Diego and try again."

"That's good enough for me. Let's go get our stuff and head home." Lukas relaxed a bit. He accepted that this was the best option for everyone, but he couldn't deny the throbbing pain growing in his chest.

He started the car. She placed her hand on his when he moved to shift the car into gear. "Morning will be soon enough. I really want you and your father to clear the air. He really did think he was helping."

Lukas laughed without a hint of mirth. "Let's just agree to disagree there. But you are right. I need to run through I few things with my Pops before I have to kill him."

SUNNY WALKED INTO THE house and immediately ran upstairs without saying anything to Lukas's father. Lukas followed her in and closed the door behind him. He took a deep breath before walking down the hallway leading into the kitchen. Lukas found his father sitting at the small kitchenette table that has been in the bay window of their kitchen for more than twenty years. He looked small and tired, holding the same navy blue coffee cup he'd used religiously for years.

"Why would you bring Sunny here? What could you have possibly been thinking?" Lukas asked the only question that still remained on his mind. He sat heavily in the seat across from his father. He honestly wasn't sure if he would be able to forgive him for what he saw as a betrayal, but he felt he should at least give him a chance to explain himself.

"I won't let you ruin your life with Emmalyn the way I ruined my life with your mother," was all Pop said as he stood and walked out the room.

Lukas watched him go. He thought about following him and asking him to explain what he meant by that. Lukas was very well aware that his parents' marriage was a complete and total disaster. He also knew that his father was left a broken man because of how it ended. His mother's suicide nearly killed his father, but he was able to hold on because Lukas and his younger brother needed him. And now Lukas felt beholden to his father because his father needed him. He knew the guilt he carried over his mother's death wasn't real. He was a toddler and had nothing to do with his mother's unhappiness. But in the back of Lukas's mind, he always felt that if he hadn't been born, his mother wouldn't have killed herself and his parents could have gone their separate ways, no harm done.

Lukas had long since understood that his father's dislike for Emmalyn was rooted in the fact that she reminded his father so much of his mother. She had the same ambitious attitude and need for order (or so he'd been told). And though his father might deny the fact until his dying day, he knew that his father had adored the woman he married and had not loved another woman since. Perhaps the reason he preferred Sunny was that he knew that Lukas would never love Sunny to the extent that he loved Emmy. But the difference was that Emmalyn didn't want him, plain and simple as that. On the car ride back to his father's house, he had convinced himself that making a life with Sunny was the smart thing to do. She was a phenomenal woman and would make the perfect wife and mother.

Lukas rose from the table and walked to the stairs. He took a deep breath and began the climb, prepared to do whatever necessary to make things right with the one woman who wanted him but wasn't really the woman he wanted.

10   Reckoning, of A Sort

IT HAD BEEN TWO months to the day since Emmalyn had last seen or spoken to either Lukas or Grant. Emmalyn's resolve to stay away from both men had grown stronger with each passing day. After her interlude with Lukas, Em couldn't bring herself to call Grant. Eventually, he'd taken the hint and stopped calling. And except for this horrible stomach flu she couldn't seem to get rid of, her mind and her life seemed to be lightening significantly. Apparently she just needed to accept that she needed to be alone a little longer. She focused on getting herself together, getting healthy, getting — something.

Em stepped out of the bathroom stall she'd just been throwing up in and washed her face off with one of the rough, brown towels in the dispenser. She swished a little water in her mouth and spit it out, hoping to hide the fact that she was still sick. Isabel and Zavia had been bugging her for over a week to go to a doctor to make sure there wasn't something more seriously wrong than the stomach flu. Em had lost quite a bit of weight and was beginning to feel light-headed at the simplest tasks. She took a look at her ashen face in the mirror and made a promise to herself that if she wasn't better by the end of the week, she would go see the doctor. Even she had to admit that she looked terrible.

She took two steps toward the door and felt her legs buckle under her. Luckily she was able to catch herself by grabbing ahold of the counter top.

"This is crazy," she thought to herself. She pulled herself upright and slowly made her way out the bathroom and back to her office. Isabel and Zavia jumped to their feet in shock and concern at her appearance. She held up her hand to cut them off before they could henpeck her to death.

"I know, I know. I'm going home. I'll go to the doctor tomorrow. I swear it. I feel awful, and it's not getting any better," she croaked out.

She slowly made her way to her desk to grab her purse and keys. She didn't even bother trying to pack her laptop. Then she handed her keys to Zavia. "Can you drive me home? I really don't think I'd make it if I tried." Emmalyn tried to smile, but the motion made her stomach drop. She barely made it to the garbage can before beginning to dry heave again. She had nothing left in her stomach to throw up.

"Are you sure we shouldn't just take you to the emergency room? You look terrible."

"No. Please, just take me home. I usually feel okay in the morning. It's just after lunch that I feel like shit. Isabel can follow in her car and drop you at your car. Please."

Isabel and Zavia exchanged worried looks, but in the end, they agreed to take Em at her word that she would go to the doctor first thing in the morning.

Before leaving, Zavia made Em promise that she would call her if she didn't feel like driving in the morning or if she began to feel worse that evening. Em promised, though she would have promised just about anything to be able to get into her bed and go to sleep.

Em walked in the house and immediately headed for the kitchen. True to her word and because her inner hypochondriac was going nuts, she grabbed the phone and made an emergency appointment with her doctor for the next morning. She then grabbed her saltines and a big glass of water and went to bed. She'd worry about not having finished her will in the morning, if she lived through the night.

Emmalyn spent exactly three hours at the doctor's office. Fifteen minutes were spent drawing blood and waiting for the doctor to tell her how much longer she had to live. Two hours and forty-five minutes were spent reviving Emmalyn and making sure she was okay to drive after her doctor told her she wasn't dying, and that she was, instead, pregnant.

EMMALYN SPENT THE NEXT three days in bed. She refused to answer her phone, respond to texts, or open her door when her concerned friends stopped by. On the fourth day, Emmalyn's sickness went away completely, and her appetite was back in full force. She dragged herself down to the kitchen to find the pantry and the refrigerator completely bare of anything but alcohol. It dawned on her that she really hadn't eaten in days and hadn't had a proper meal in weeks. Her hand instinctively went to her belly. Her mind hadn't accepted the truth of her condition, but her body had. She went back to her bedroom, arguing with herself about whether she should order food in or head to the grocery store. She had no clue what pregnant women ate. She tried to remember what Zavia ate while pregnant, but all she could remember was that Zavia had an intense and overwhelming need for eggnog—damned inconvenient too, since Zee's first trimester had occurred during the spring of the year.

Finally deciding to order something and hit the grocery store, she called an Indian restaurant that wasn't too far from her house and ordered several different entrees. They all sounded good, but she wasn't sure what she would be able to hold down. As she threw on some presentably clean clothes and ran a brush through her hair (dear God, when was the last time I combed my hair, she thought, as the brush got caught in yet another knot), she made a quick list of necessities and headed out to the store.

She grabbed her purse, remembering that the doctor had given her some pamphlets about healthy pregnancy as well as a referral to an obstetrician. She pulled the first pamphlet out. It was titled A Joyous Time and had a picture of a happy couple and a cute baby. The sight of the man in the picture instantly brought the father of the child she was carrying to the front of her mind, the one she'd taken to bed then let walk out of her house and her life. Emmalyn threw the pamphlet on the table, grabbed her keys, and headed out the door.

Unable to wait until getting home to begin eating, she grabbed a piece of buttery naan from the box on top. She munched on the delicious flatbread as she drove home. Isabel and Zavia were sitting on her stoop waiting for her.

"Dammit," she cursed to herself.

Emmalyn wasn't ready to have this conversation with herself, let alone her two best friends. Em pulled into her driveway and grabbed the food off the front seat.

Zavia rushed over to her, blocking her in the doorway of the car. "Where in the hell have you been? I have been trying to reach you for days now," she charged.

"I'm fine. I'm not dying." Emmalyn smiled and tried to move around Zavia, but Zavia was having none of Emmalyn's flippant attitude.

"Emmalyn, I swear I am about this close to beating the shit out of you right here. Now what in the entire fuck is going on with you? Missing work? Not answering your phones, texts, emails? I'm worried about you." Zavia began to tear up, illustrating just how worried about her friend she'd really been.

Em blushed in guilt and embarrassment. "I know you are. I know you both are. But please, give me some time, and I'll tell you everything. I'm just not ready to talk about it yet."

"What about work?" Isabel asked. Since they'd generally partnered up on most of their projects, Isabel had been covering Emmalyn's share of the work, but that was getting tiresome.

"I've taken a short leave of absence. I talked to HR and Martin and they've agreed to two weeks." Emmalyn couldn't quite meet Isabel's eyes. She knew she should have told Isabel directly, but she wanted to avoid just this kind of confrontation. Isabel simply walked away. She took her purse off the stairs and headed toward the car she and Zavia had ridden in.

Zavia turned on Emmalyn, anger pulsating in her eyes and in her voice. "You have one week to tell me what is going on with you, or so help me God, I will do you harm. Do you hear me? You push our friendship too far sometimes." Zavia turned away, not giving Emmalyn a chance to respond. Em couldn't do anything but stare as the two people who had always been there for her, no matter what, drove away in anger.

"Why didn't I just tell them," she thought to herself as she unpacked her car and carried her food and groceries into the house. But she knew exactly why. She didn't want them to know she'd slept with Lukas and that she was now going to be having his child. But she was going to have to fess up, and soon. And not just to Isabel and Zavia.

ZAVIA PACED THE FLOOR anxiously. Their planned intervention with Emmalyn did not go as planned. If anything, the encounter left Zavia even more worried than before. Back at Isabel's apartment, it was obvious that Isabel was more hurt by Em's behavior than she'd let on. Zavia sat next to her on the sofa, patting her back in what she hoped was a comforting way.

"She doesn't mean to be this oblivious and stupid. She just is," Zavia stated matter-of-factly.

Isabel just sighed in resignation. "I know. The work is piling up and I can't keep up. Em was the workaholic, not me. I did the meetings; she cranked out the code. I'm dying here," she disclosed.

"Can't you sweet-talk someone into helping you with some of the work? I bet that dude from commercial IT would jump at the chance to help you out." Zavia giggled and wiggled her eyebrows suggestively.

Isabel smiled. "I just wish I knew what was going on with her. If it's not worth all this drama, I'm going to kill her."

"Me too. And I've known her longer, so I get first dibs. I checked with Lukas's company. He's back in California, so that's not it."

"Maybe things went south with Grant again?"

Zavia jumped up and started pacing again. "Who knows? I've got to get home. I meant what I told her. She has a week to pull her head out of her ass, or I'm going to pull it out for her." She grabbed her purse and headed for the door. She paused with her hand on the knob and turned back to Isabel. "It's going to be okay. I promise."

Isabel gave Zavia a weak smile. "Thanks, Zee. Tell my boy I'll be at his game this weekend. He's getting better every game."

"I know," Zavia beamed. "Mommy's little baller. Lord knows he didn't get athletic ability from his dad. I'll see you there."

On the car ride home, Zavia had a nagging feeling in her gut that she knew what was going on with Emmalyn. She didn't want to push, but there was definitely something off about Em that she couldn't quite put her finger on. She almost drove through her garage door as the realization of what that something was hit her square in the chest.

11 Come To Jesus

EMMALYN DIDN'T NEED THE full week of Zavia's ultimatum to come to terms with her situation. At her first OB-GYN appointment, they gave her an ultra-sound, and she was able to hear the baby's heartbeat. That was all it took for her to fall in love with the child she was carrying. As she walked out of the doctor's office, she called Zavia and then Isabel and asked them to meet her for dinner.

She went home and gave herself a full pampering treatment — long bath, wash and set for her hair, and polish for her nails. She arrived at the restaurant early and ordered appetizers to munch while she waited. Suddenly, she was excited to let her friends in on her secret.

Zavia arrived first. She looked harried and concerned. Emmalyn felt bad for holding her friends at bay, but she couldn't deal with their hovering and finding out about the baby. Isabel came in a few minutes later. After both sat down and put in their drink orders with the cute waiter who didn't know who to flirt with first, Em took her friends' hands in hers.

"I am so sorry for being a selfish, self-absorbed shit the last couple of weeks. I'm going to explain, but it comes in two separate-but-related confessions. I need you both to promise to hear me out before you start fussing, okay?"

She waited for each to nod before continuing. She took a deep breath and a drink of water before going on. "The night I had the date with Grant, Lukas interrupted us. He and Brian came in, and despite my repeated pleas to be left alone, he insisted that he needed to say his piece. Brian finally dragged him out, but he'd already ruined the date. I asked Grant to leave me at the restaurant, and I had planned to take a cab home since that was how I'd gotten there. When I left, Lukas was waiting for me. I let him drive me home, and one thing led to another."

Zavia cursed under her breath. Isabel simply sat stunned. Emmalyn pushed on. "The day I left the office sick, I did make the appointment with my doctor. She told me I was pregnant. When you two caught me in front of my house, I wasn't ready to talk about it yet, but then I went to the OB-GYN and heard the baby's heartbeat. It was the most amazing thing I'd ever heard. So, there you have it. I'm gonna be a mama."

Zavia and Isabel sat speechless. Zavia kept blinking, but no sound came out of her mouth.

"I see," Isabel said. "Does this mean you're coming back to work though?"

Emmalyn did a double take, unsure she'd heard Isabel correctly. "Yeah. I'll be there first thing Monday morning.

"Good, because your to-do list is long," Isabel muttered, trying in vain to cover her surprise.

Emmalyn laughed softly. She looked over to Zavia, who still hadn't spoken.

"Please, Zee, I need to know you are okay with this."

"Okay with this? Okay? Of course I'm not okay! We asked, we begged, we demanded you stay away from him. Now you sit there all giddy and ridiculous and tell us you're pregnant? Are you shitting me? You can't take care of a baby. You're a fucking disaster," Zavia bellowed.

Emmalyn blinked to keep the tears from falling. It had never occurred to her that her oldest friend would have reacted this harshly. She knew Zavia would disapprove, but this? Never this.

"I'm sorry," she whispered. "I made a mistake. But I am overjoyed about this baby. Don't worry, Little Miss Perfection, I won't bother you with it." Emmalyn slammed her napkin on the table and stormed out the restaurant, Zavia hot on her heels.

Zavia caught her by the arm as the reached the sidewalk. "Don't you dare try to act hurt. You always do this. Get yourself in some kind of mess and expect us to be happy about it. What were you thinking?"

"I'm pregnant, Zavia. It happens, even to walking disasters like me. The baby and I will be fine."

"Jesus, Em, what about your depression, huh? The medications can't be good for the baby? Fuck it all, Emmalyn -- what about Lukas?" Zavia questioned. "Is he going to be happy about this too?"

Em skipped over Zee's questions about her depression and her meds. She and the doctor had been round and round about what precautions she should be taking. Lukas, however, was another matter all together. "Lukas is in California," Em hissed tightly through clenched teeth.

"He is the baby's father, right? He has a right to know," Zavia pointed out.

"He doesn't have a right to shit! God, you are so high and mighty. I'm sorry to disappoint you yet again, Zavia, but I am a disaster, just like you said. A manic-depressive clusterfuck. But I'll be goddamned if I'm going to let Lukas do to this child what my father did to me. You breathe a word of this to him and I will never forgive you!" Emmalyn spun on her heel and went back inside the restaurant, leaving Zavia standing gape-mouthed on the sidewalk, trying to decide what she wanted to do next.

"TRY NOT TO BE too angry with Zee. She's just worried about you," Isabel said when Em flopped down in the chair. She racked her mind for something to say that wouldn't make the situation worse. Nothing came to her.

Em picked up her glass and swirled the icy water around a bit, furious and hurt. "That's not what it sounded like to me, Isabel. It sounded like she was being a judgmental bitch who knows what's best for everyone and can't accept that we're not all some fucking annoying cross between Mary Poppins and superwoman like she is," she complained.

"I'm not superwoman," Zavia chimed in from behind Em's chair. "I know I act like I have it all together, but I really don't. I just hate seeing you get hurt, Em. You're my best friend. I'm sorry for how I reacted." She sat down at the table and took a healthy drink from her wine glass.

"Zavia, I'm not trying to ruin my life or Lukas's. I wasn't going to say anything to him. He has his life in California; my life is here. We agreed—one night, no questions, no strings. It's better this way," Em insisted.

Isabel's eyes were wide with disbelief. "You're not going to tell him? Shouldn't he know?"

"Probably, but all we ever do is hurt each other. I don't want to put the baby in the middle of our issues. I can't help that I'm pregnant, and I'm sure as hell not getting rid of it. But I can try my best to mitigate the drama as much as possible."

Zavia wanted to argue the complete wrongness of Emmalyn's attitude, but all she said was, "If that's your decision, we'll support you."

"Really? Because despite my earlier declarations, I'm totally gonna need you guys," Em sheepishly admitted.

Isabel took Emmalyn's hand in her own and gave her a reassuring smile. "Of course we think you're absolutely wrong, but you're our girl. And that baby is going to have two of the most annoyingly loving aunties ever."

Zavia's smile turned sinister. "Oh, I am totally going to pay you back for every gram of sugar you have ever given Jared, and I am going to seriously enjoy it!"

"Oh Lord." Em rolled her eyes and snatched up another piece of bread.

The three friends dissolved into a fit of giggles and baby planning. Over the course of dinner, Zavia delighted in describing, in excruciating and disgusting detail, what pregnancy and childbirth were like for her. Isabel threatened more than once to throw-up right there at the table.

And despite the return to easiness, Emmalyn wasn't comfortable sharing the fears she had about impending motherhood and her decision not to tell Lukas about their child. She knew full well she was wrong but wasn't able to bring herself to talk to him.

"So, I'm going to Arizona to visit my mom this weekend," Emmalyn blurted out.

"You are willingly going to step foot in Delma's house?" Zavia was reasonably skeptical of this plan. Emmalyn and her mother'd had a rough relationship since her father's death. Zavia couldn't remember the last time Em had even mentioned her mother in conversation.

"I mean, yeah, you know. With the baby coming, it's about time I mend fences with her. Don't you think?" Em tried to smile enough to look like she was confident in what she was saying. The truth was the complete opposite. She didn't want to see her mother and definitely didn't want to lay her faults open for her mother to rip her to shreds. But she needed someone to talk to, and her mother was going to have to suffice.

So why did she suddenly feel like she was going to be sick?

12   HOMECOMING... SORTA

EMMALYN SAT IN HER rental car outside of her mother's clean beige stucco house in Yuma, Arizona, and contemplated driving back to North Carolina. She knew she was being ridiculous, but she was really not interested in being subjected to the high level of irrationality her mother could achieve in a relatively short amount of time. On the plane ride west, she'd convinced herself that her mother could surprise her and just be a normal, reassuring mom for once. A flash of something shiny in her peripheral vision caught her eye. As she slowly turned her head to see what it was, she knew she couldn't have been more wrong.

Em watched the beautiful middle-aged woman rush down her driveway toward the car. Her mother hadn't aged a day in the last three years. She had the same medium- brown skin, and sparkling, brown, almost-black eyes that Emmalyn remembered. Her hair had been cut short, and the gray had been color rinsed away. It was what she was wearing, however, that drew Em's attention. Her mother had on a gold lamé jumpsuit that looked like it had been taken straight off some disco dancer in 1976. It was, quite simply, ridiculous. Em's head fell forward, and she banged it twice on the steering wheel before opening the car door and stepping out.

"Well, what are you doing just sitting in the car in this heat? Come on inside!" Delma grabbed her daughter and pulled her into a tight hug. Em found herself caught up in her mother's enthusiasm and hugged her back. She even managed to smile.

"Mom, what on earth are you wearing? And why are you out in public in it?" Emmalyn asked, laughing.

Delma put her arm through Emmalyn's and led her to the house. "This is my workout outfit. You can't tell me I don't look hot, honey."

Em and Delma walked into the house amiably enough. Emmalyn followed her mother through the living room and into the kitchen. The room was crammed with tchotchkes and souvenirs. On a wall near the kitchen was a space dedicated to pictures of Em growing up. Her mother still had every school picture Em had had taken over the years. There were collages of candid shots of Emmalyn and her dad too. Em was stunned. She couldn't believe her mom had kept them all. Despite having divorced Em's father before his death, Delma and Ray had stayed very close. She still had each of their annual family portraits hanging on the wall.

"I still can't let him go, you know." Delma stood in the doorway watching the emotions pass over her daughter's face.

"I see. Bobby is okay with pictures of your dead ex-husband on his den wall?"

"He has no choice but to be okay with it. Besides, it's not like I can cheat or anything. Your dad was my soulmate. No matter how things ended, I loved that man with everything I was. Even still, I talk to his pictures because I like to pretend I can still talk to him."

"Even after everything he put you through, put us through, you still loved him?"

"Your heart will continue to love no matter what your brain says, baby girl. My brain knew he wasn't any good for either of us, but my heart couldn't beat as long as he and I were apart. When he died, I thought I was going to die too. I felt every thump of my heartbeat, felt it like an old engine trying to turn over. I had lost my other half. But I held on, for you, for your sake, because you needed a mama, though I'm guessing the argument can be made that I wasn't a very good one."

"I know you did the best you could. You just seemed so lost, and I was too young to be able to help you. I felt so frustrated. Eventually, I turned away."

"Well, you're here now. So, how about some lunch?"

"That depends. Are you back to eating normal black-people food again?"

"Black people can be vegan, thank you very much, but it just so happens that I am back on eating meat. How about some pulled-pork and cole slaw?"

Emmalyn's smile was a mile wide. She loved her mother's homemade pulled pork and cole slaw. "You know I am not mad with that!"

They sat down and ate. It was as if the last ten years hadn't happened, and the specter of her father's broken life wasn't still haunting them. Emmalyn re-laxed, truly relaxed, for the first time in weeks.

The meal complete, mother and daughter adjourned to the back patio. The air was warm but dry. Em loved it.

"So, what brings you all the way to Arizona?"

Em took a deep breath. She wasn't sure she was ready to tell her mother what had brought her to town. Then again, she wasn't sure she would ever real-ly be ready. "I'm pregnant."

Delma nodded slowly. "Huh. I see. Am I happy or sad at the news?"

Emmalyn frowned, then laughed, understanding dawning slowly. "I hope you're happy."

"Good. Because I'm ecstatic. I can't wait to be a grandma!" Delma pulled Em over to her side of the deck sofa and hugged her tight.

Emmalyn began tearing up, and before she could stop herself, she'd gone full blubber. "Oh, Mom. I've made such a mess of things."

"Oh, ok, so happy with a caveat. What's the mess you made?" probed Delma gently.

"The baby is Lukas's. He was in town for work. We hooked up, and now I'm having his baby."

"Huh. I see. And are we happy or sad at that bit of news?" she asked slowly, not wanting to cause ripples or set her daughter off.

"I don't know, Ma." Emmalyn pulled away from her mother and stood up. She paced the length of the deck over and again. Delma watched and waited. Emmalyn had always had a need to come to things in her own time. She knew better than to push Em too hard. "I've decided I'm not going to tell him about the baby."

"Why on earth not? It's his responsibility too," Delma asked, catching herself before launching into a full lecture.

Em looked truly pathetic. "He has his own life in California. Too much time has passed, too much pain between us to go back. It was a mistake. I don't want to compound it by forcing a relationship with someone who isn't right for me."

"Uh huh."

"What uh huh?" Em stopped pacing and turned to face her mother.

"Well, baby girl, this is pretty tricky territory. On the one hand, I don't want you to be mad with me anymore and not let me see my grandbaby. But on the other hand, I don't want to have to lie to you. So you get uh huh."

Emmalyn sat in one of the chairs across from the sofa. Her pants were tight and uncomfortable, partly from overeating at lunch, partly because she didn't have any maternity clothes. She wriggled in the chair until she found a comfortable position. "Just give it to me. I won't get mad."

"Promise?"

"I swear." She held up her hand in an oath.

"You and Lukas remind me so much of me and your father. It's why I never really supported your relationship with him. Your father was the sweetest, kindest, most thoughtful man on the planet, but his head was always in the clouds, never on the task at hand. And if it wasn't in the clouds, it was in the bottom of a bottle of bourbon. And I never cared. I thought I could always be responsible enough for both of us. I always had to be the adult, and, frankly, that get's tiresome.

"I know Lukas never drank, but his head was always somewhere else, and he always seemed to leave you holding the bag somewhere. And it scared me because I know what happens when the adults lose their patience, when the rose-colored lenses come off. And I never wanted that for you. But despite everything, I wouldn't trade your time with your father for anything."

"Really? Because I would. He was never there. He constantly made promises he knew damn well he couldn't keep. He missed recitals, ball games, ceremonies. It broke my heart every time I looked in the crowd and saw that empty seat next to you."

"Your daddy loved you," Delma asserted. It broke her heart to think that Em didn't know just how much her daddy had loved her.

"I know. He told me ten times a day. But he was never there when I needed him, and neither was Lukas. I won't let him do that to this baby—not if I can help it."

"Lukas deserves a chance to try. You aren't God. You can't decide who gets to be a parent and who doesn't. I'm not trying to hurt you, but what if Lukas decided you weren't going to be a good mother and tried to take the baby away from you? Would that be fair? Of course not. Because you will be an amazing mother. And he will be an amazing father. Or he won't. But your baby deserves the chance to have a father in its life. I'll stand by you no matter what, but I hope you'll think about what I'm saying."

Delma stood up and kissed Em on the forehead. "I'm so glad you came. I've missed you so much. You just don't know, baby girl."

Em smiled. "I missed you too," she replied, surprised to find that she meant it. "What time does Bobby get home?"

Delma waved her hand in dismissal. "I sent him off fishing. It's just us girls this weekend."

AFTER TOSSING AND TURNING most of the night, Emmalyn's brain came to a decision somewhere around four a.m. She waited until she heard Delma moving around before getting up and tracking her down. She finally found her mother sitting on the back porch sipping coffee and reading the front page of the newspaper. She jumped when Emmalyn came bursting out of the sliding glass door.

"Emmalyn," Delma exclaimed. "What's got you up so early? It's not the baby is it?"

"No. Get dressed. We're going on a road trip."

"Oh. Okay. Where are we going?"

"California. I've got an ex to track down."

"Emmy, I don't think...," her mother started but then thought better of it. "I'll go get dressed."

She set her coffee down and stood up. Emmalyn pulled her into an awkward but strong hug. "Thanks, Mom."

It took about two hours for mother and daughter to finally leave the house. It was easy to find Lukas's address on the Internet. Emmalyn wasn't sure about bringing her mother along, but that issue solved itself about halfway into the ride from Yuma to San Diego when Delma announced that although she was tagging along for moral support, she didn't think it was wise for her to be there for the actual conversation.

"You two are adults, and you'll have to develop a way to communicate with each other and not be angry or accusatory. It's up to you to set the tone, baby girl. Men are emotional creatures. They don't have the capacity to be rational and logical. Set the terms you want, and negotiate from there."

"I'm pretty sure that's exactly what they say about us," Em replied laughing. She shifted in her seat for the umpteenth time. "I have got to get new pants. These are cutting off the circulation to my feet."

Delma laughed. "When I got pregnant with you, I couldn't fit into any of my clothes after about a month. I had at least three different wardrobes because I didn't think it was possible for me to get any bigger. And, oh Lord, the heartburn. Don't even get me started on that."

The mindless baby chatter helped calm Emmalyn's mind. More than once she contemplated turning around and simply calling him when she got back to Charlotte. But her conscience wouldn't let her. She had to see this, through and she wasn't going to let the massive number of butterflies trying to flit their way through her stomach stop her.

13 Well Damn

EMMALYN DIDN'T GIVE HERSELF a chance to talk herself out of the conversation. She barely got the car into park before jumping out.

"Good luck, sweetheart," her mother called before going back to the thick novel she'd brought with her.

She didn't see any cars in the drive but rang the bell anyway. Then she took a step back from the door, not wanting to seem overly enthusiastic.

The woman who answered the door was simply breathtaking. She was at least four inches taller than Emmalyn, with smooth, caramel-colored skin and a smattering of freckles across her nose and cheeks. The woman's hair was at least down the center of her back, all curls and half-tamed, reddish-brown wildness. Emmalyn was awestruck.

The woman smiled. Her voice was something beyond melodic. "Can I help you?"

Emmalyn needed a couple of seconds to find her own voice. "Um, well, I was looking for Lukas."

"I see. He isn't home." The woman's smile faltered, and her head fell to one side as recognition lit her eyes. "You're Emmalyn, aren't you?"

"Yes, I am. I just wanted to tell Lukas something, but it isn't important." Em couldn't hold the woman's gaze. She felt like a complete idiot.

"Why don't you come in? Lukas won't be back for a while, but I'd like to talk to you." Sunny swept her arm in a wide arc, offering Em entry into the house before she could argue.

"Um," Emmalyn's voice cracked as she stalled for time. She quickly looked around for something she could use as an means of escape. Her feet weren't helping the situation. No way she wanted to go in the house with this gorgeous creature. But she'd clearly violated the woman's home and felt she owed her that much. "Sure," Emmalyn replied, "okay."

The house was beautiful. There was clearly a woman's touch in the decorating. The Lukas Emmalyn had known was perfectly happy with futons and egg crates.

This house looked like something out of one of Zavia's interior design magazines.

"Please, have a seat."

"I'd rather not. My mom is out in the car, and we're going to the beach before we head back to Arizona."

"So, you live in Arizona now?" Sunny asked, obviously not believing one word of Em's hastily cobbled together story.

"No, my mother and her husband live in Yuma. We were heading to the beach. I figured I'd to stop by and say hi," she added, hoping to add credibility to the story.

"I see. I want you to know that I know about you and Lukas's last visit, and I've forgiven the transgression. We are going to be married in a month."

Emmalyn couldn't hide her surprise. She'd specifically asked him if there was someone else, and he'd said no. "I didn't know that," was all she could get out. Her mind raced a hundred miles an hour.

"I can see that. I am well aware that the man I'm marrying is still in love with someone else, but he is under the impression that there is no chance for reconciliation between you. Does your visit here today mean he read you wrong?" Sunny's perfectly arched eyebrows were raised in clear anticipation of Em's response.

"Nope. He was absolutely right on that point. There is not a snowball's chance in hell of a reconciliation,"

Em said growing angrier by the second. "I was simply in the area and wanted to say hi. I thought we were still friends. I can see that I was wrong. I am so sorry for coming here, and you can rest assured that I will never do so again." Emmalyn was furious and embarrassed and very eager to be away from this place. She never should have come here, and now she had absolute proof that her initial assessment of Lukas was correct. He didn't deserve any consideration from her.

Sunny didn't say anything. It was clear that Emmalyn had no clue she existed and was beyond furious at finding out this way. It didn't matter to her. Whatever the reason, Emmalyn wasn't going to be reaching out to Lukas again, and that was just fine by her.

Emmalyn's hand was on the doorknob when she turned back to Sunny with fire burning in her eyes. "Please don't tell Lukas I was here. He doesn't need to know."

"It'll stay just between us girls," Sunny replied, all smiles.

As Emmalyn left Lukas and Sunny's life behind, she was on the verge of tears. She didn't say a word to her mother as she jumped in the car and slammed the door shut. Out of the corner of her eye, she saw a car pulling into the driveway. But as the tears fell, she didn't care enough to turn around.

LUKAS NEARLY CRASHED INTO a parked car as he watched Emmalyn storming away from his house and peeling away in a strange car. He sat in the driveway trying decide if he wanted to follow Emmalyn or go inside and face Sunny. Despite the strong desire to go after Em, he had no clue where Em was going and didn't think he'd be able to find her. Instead, he opted to face Sunny and the ass-chewing he knew was waiting for him. She met him at the door, having watched his struggle from the window.

She stepped out onto the stoop, head cocked to one side. Her smile wasn't friendly.

"Couldn't decide who to go to first? Seriously?" She turned and went back into the house, headed straight for the master bedroom. "So, what, you came in here because you didn't know where she was going?" she threw over her shoulder.

She'd struck him right in the truth. He hung his head, disgusted with himself. "Sunny, I didn't know she was coming."

"I am well aware of that." She turned on him suddenly. "Why didn't she know about me? Why didn't she know you were getting married? Why didn't you tell her?"

"I don't know. I—I didn't know what to say," he said weakly.

"Are you kidding me?" Sunny slapped him across his face. "Lukas, come on, be real with me. You ran into a woman you were clearly not over. You slept with her. At no point did it ever cross your mind that you'd given me a ring, made a commitment to me?"

"Sunny, please. It was one night. No conversation, no strings, no promises. She asked me if there was someone else, and I said no. I wanted what she was offering, and I knew if I told her the truth, she would have kicked me out. I don't know why she was here," he defended, albeit poorly.

"I don't care why she was here. I want to know why she looked like I had punched her in the gut when I told her we were going to be married in a month. And I gotta tell you, if you'd been here, I'm pretty sure she would have beaten the shit out of you—she was that angry."

"I can only imagine. Emmalyn has a very short temper. She didn't yell at you did she?"

Sunny rolled her eyes. "Thanks for your concern, but she was very cordial as I pulled the rug from under her feet." She shook her head in disbelief. She then pulled her engagement ring off and set it on the dresser.

"Sunny, please don't do that. This will work." He knew as soon as the words were out of his mouth how grossly untrue they were. This wasn't ever going to work.

"It shouldn't have to work. It should be. You should be looking at me the way you look at her. I saw you. I watched your face as you realized who she was. I saw the distress you felt at not being able to go after her. I can't be Emmalyn, and I can't be some consolation prize, Lukas. I thought I was okay with it because I wanted the life we've been building, the life you promised me. But this isn't right." Sunny fought the tears that had been building behind her eyes. Clearly, Emmalyn wasn't the only one to have the rug pulled out from under her today.

"Sunny, I am so sorry. This isn't what I wanted. You don't have to go."

"You'll let me keep your house," she laughed. "No thanks. I don't need to live among the life I can't have. Can you give me a few days to find somewhere else to go?"

"Take all the time you need. I'll stay at a hotel this weekend." He took a chance and stepped toward her. When she didn't cringe, he pulled her into a hug. "I am so sorry. You deserve better than this."

As she moved away from him, she smirked and said, "Well, don't think I'm all charity. Even though you won't have me standing in the way, your precious Emmalyn is never going to forgive you for not being straight up with her. I could see it in her eyes."

"You're probably right. But I think I have to try."

14 PITCHING A FIT

"OKAY, HOW ABOUT THIS one?" Isabel and Em-malyn were deeply engrossed in the pages of a baby furniture catalog. Em had been back at work for a week. During the drive back to Yuma, Delma was able to provide some perspective. Emmalyn hadn't told Lukas about the baby, but since he hadn't told her about his fiancé, she thought they were even. Let him stay in California and be with his new wife. Emmalyn would be just fine. She decided not to tell Zavia and Isabel about her side trip. She didn't need them adding to the angry voices in her head.

"Too fancy. If the baby is as clumsy as I am, it'll just get its head stuck in between the slats." Isabel laughed, and Em swatted at her with the book. "You weren't supposed to laugh. You were supposed to say, 'Hey, you're not a klutz.' Jeez."

"You want me to lie to you?" Isabel tried to stifle her laughs, but it was a waste of time. Em couldn't walk across carpet without stumbling at least twice.

"Yes. Aren't you supposed to be sensitive to pregnant women?"

"Oh Lord, do not start that crap."

The phone rang, cutting off their banter. Isabel picked it up, ducking a flying pen.

"We'll be right there," she said sharply before hanging up the phone. "New client is here. Gotta get back on the grind."

"Fine. I need to get some water first. I'll meet you in there."

Emmalyn went to the kitchen and refilled her water bottle. She was walking while taking a deep drink as she turned into the conference room, running smack into Isabel's back.

"Sorry, Isabel, I...." Her voice faltered as she spotted her new clients. Lukas and Brian sat next to each other at the far end of the conference table. Database schemas and design documents littered the table. Brian at least had the good manners to look sorry for his part in this disaster.

Isabel tried to compose herself, but her head simply swung between Lukas and Emmalyn. Lukas looked genuinely afraid, and Emmalyn looked purely homicidal. "Em, why don't you go back to the office, and I'll get rid of them."

"We have a legitimate business need. This is a real meeting," Brian implored, his voice oddly strained.

Isabel shot Brian a look that made him squirm in his chair. "You have got to be shitting me," she whispered angrily.

He held his hands up and nodded toward Lukas.

"I'm not doing this. Find another UI developer." Emmalyn turned on her heel and walked quickly back to her office. Lukas was prepared for her to run and was after her before she could get out of the room. He followed her, but because he didn't remember where her office was, he almost walked past her door. He got his hand in the door just as she went to slam it, catching it squarely on his palm. Out of instinct, she pulled the door open, and he pushed his way in, closing the door behind him.

"Get out of my office," Em said, quickly sitting behind her desk. She was definitely showing and didn't want him to notice it.

"Why did you come to San Diego? I thought you said no strings."

"And there aren't any. I was in Arizona visiting my mother, and we went to San Diego to hit the beach. I just wanted to say hi."

"So, why did you leave? Why not wait until I got home to say hi?"

She looked at him incredulously. "Because I didn't realize you had a roommate. I'm sorry, fiancée," she said with an angry sneer. "I asked you. I specifically asked you if there was someone else, and you looked me dead in my face and said no. What kind of asshole does that?"

"Emmalyn, you don't understand." This wasn't going the way he'd planned. He'd convinced himself that since Em had come to San Diego, she clearly wanted to reconcile. The angry woman standing before him looked more prepared to kill him and hide his body parts in the river.

Em stood up and walked around the desk. They were no more than six inches apart; instinctively, he took a step back. "I'm going to stop you right there," she ground out. "I understand completely. I was offering you sex. You wanted the sex, and you lied to make sure I didn't change my mind. That makes me stupid and you a fucking pig!"

The door cracked open slowly and Isabel stuck her hand in, waving it around to get their attention. Next came her head. "So, yeah, these walls aren't nearly as thick as one would think, so everyone still in the office can hear everything you're saying. Just a heads up." She slipped back out and closed the door behind her.

"Get out of my office. Go back to California and stay there. I swear I will never come looking for you again. Please. Just go."

She noticed he wasn't listening to her anymore. His face went slack, and his eyes shifted back and forth between the catalog on her desk and her midsection. She tried to skirt around him and back behind the relative safety of her desk, but he caught her by the arm.

"Are you pregnant?" Lukas demanded.

She didn't answer. She pulled her arm away and sat back down behind her desk, shoving the catalog under a stack of papers.

"Answer me, Emmalyn. Are you pregnant?"

She didn't look at him, instead bored holes in her hands. "Yes," she whispered, barely audible.

"Is it my baby or the dude I saw you at dinner with?"

She looked up at him, red hot anger etched all over her face. "Excuse me?" she yelled, jumping awkwardly out of her chair.

"It's a fair question. But judging from your reaction, I'll venture a guess that it's mine." He took another step back in anticipation of her taking a swing at his head. His eyes lost their focus, and he slumped down into the chair across from her desk. He compulsively ran his hand over his face, as his mind tried to digest and understand what was happening.

Emmalyn watched Lukas process the situation. Damn him, he looked happy! She sat back down, sighed, and put her head down on her desk. "Lukas, I'm not asking for anything from you."

"Emmy, that is my kid in there," he said motioning toward her. "You don't have to ask. I want to be there for you and the baby."

"You are out of your mind. I don't want you any-where near me or my baby. Go disappoint someone else," she spat at him.

Isabel and Brian came into the office. "I didn't hear any yelling, so I thought I would be safe," Brian said. He turned to Emmalyn, his eyes and mouth pulled taut for begging and pleading. "So, we really do need to hire developers and an architect to build some soft-ware, and I'd really like to use you guys, so can we please, please, work through this requirements session, and I swear Lukas will never darken your office door-step unless or until you ask him to come by. Okay? Okay? Good."

"I expect we need to work through this baby situa-tion, Emmalyn. You can't avoid me forever," he threatened half-heartedly.

Em scoffed and laughed. "I most certainly can avoid you for at least another six-and- a-half months," she mumbled. "Let's finish this. I'm tired."

"Wait, baby situation? What baby situation?" Bri-an asked, confused.

"Don't worry about it," Isabel laughed. "You're not the father." She led Brian out of the office, giving Lu-kas and Emmalyn a few more seconds alone.

"I mean it, Emmalyn. I intend to do the right thing. Please don't shut me out. I'm sorry for lying to you about Sunny. You were right—I'm a pig. I wanted to have sex with you, and that's why I lied. But in no way am I sorry for wanting you, Emmy."

"Stop calling me that. I'm not your Emmy—not anymore," she said as she stormed past him and out of the office. Sadly accepting her statement, he followed her back to the conference room.

15 Just The Facts Ma'am

LUKAS ARRIVED AT EMMALYN'S house with a big bag of Italian food to act as a buffer. Food had always been a good way to soften Emmy up.

"Wait, can't call her Emmy," he reminded himself. He rang the bell praying she wasn't waiting on the other side with a weapon. Lukas held the food in front of his face as she opened the door.

"Peace offering," he said before she could fuss. Snatching it away as she reached for the bag, he teased, "You have to let me in to get the food."

"Smells like Italian," she said skeptically, sniffing loudly.

"Your favorite," he replied, eyebrows wiggling in invitation.

Em cocked her head to one side and crossed her arms over her chest. "And what might that be, pray tell?"

Lukas's smile slipped just a notch. He prayed silently that his memory was as strong as he thought. "Shrimp parmesan?"

She didn't move, with the exception of raising a single eyebrow. "Are you asking or telling me?"

"Telling. Now move so I can come in. The food is getting cold, and you hate cold food."

Emmalyn narrowed her eyes. "Damn it," she thought, "he remembered." Sighing loudly and dramatically, she stepped aside and let him in.

Smiling widely, Lukas walked in and headed straight for the kitchen. He was unpacking the bag as Em walked in. He noticed the slight curve of her stomach and was transfixed. Emmalyn shifted under his stare.

"What?" she asked, checking her clothing for stains or holes.

"You're starting to show. I guess I wasn't really prepared for that."

"Oh. Well. Yeah." Suddenly very self-conscious, Em sat on a stool at the counter as Lukas laid their food out.

They ate in silence. Emmalyn couldn't deny that this was a scene from her dreams many a night. When she ended things with Lukas, her heart was broken, and she was angry. She'd spent so many of her days waiting for her dad, only to be disappointed, and she couldn't and wouldn't willingly do that again. But that didn't mean she didn't love Lukas desperately. She did then, and she still did. She would have sworn she could feel the ice around her heart melt just a bit.

After their lunch, they went into the living room. Em shifted around a bit, trying to get comfortable, but Lukas kept staring at her stomach and making it difficult for her to settle down. Lukas's first statement nearly caused Em to faint. "I think we should get married," he quietly tossed out.

"Have you lost what little brains you have left?" Emmalyn was incredulous. One night of sex and now he was actually suggesting they get married. She didn't know whether to laugh or slap him. "I thought we were going to have a serious discussion. Just because you knocked me up and remembered my favorite food does not mean all is well between us."

"Em, I want our kid to have both parents. I really think we would be good parents."

Emmalyn sat in a chair and put her feet up on the coffee table. She was staring intently at her nails when she asked, "What does your fiancée think about you wanting to marry another woman? I know you don't have enough focus to be a bigamist."

"That isn't funny, Emmalyn."

"I wasn't joking, Lukas."

Lukas stood and began to pace the floor, trying to determine the best way to proceed forward. He needed to be meticulous in how he delivered his message to Em, or risk having the entire situation blow up in his face. Weighing the pros and cons, he figured he was doomed regardless, so he went straight for the heart of the matter.

"After you came to the house, Sunny left me. I couldn't give her a sufficient reason for not having told you about her or our engagement. She thought that meant that I didn't love her."

"Do you? Do you love her?" Emmalyn didn't want to know the answer to that, but she couldn't stop herself from asking. Unwillingly, she held her breath.

"Not the way I love you." There. He'd said it. And then he waited for her response.

Her eyes pierced him straight through. "And why didn't you tell me about her? It couldn't have just been the sex." Her fingers fumbled over an invisible piece of string.

He ran his hand grimly over his face then he sighed deeply. "Emmalyn, please. I don't think I can handle much more honesty today. I can accept that us getting married isn't a good idea right now." Her head popped up, but he pressed on. "But, the fact is, I'm not engaged anymore, and I want to be a part of our child's life." He paused, unsure about pressing his luck any further. He decided to lay all his cards on the table. "I want to be a part of your life."

Emmalyn fought the rising anger in her mind and her heart. "Jesus Christ, Lukas, you don't get it. You never did. I always thought you were oblivious to what I needed, but I don't know if that was the case. If you can't be honest with yourself about this, how can I believe that you are being honest with yourself about the baby? I want you to really think about what you know about me, our history, and whether or not you can be there for this child the way it will need you to. Because if you can't, I don't want you anywhere near either of us."

"Em — " He broke off when he realized Emmalyn was fighting tears.

"Lukas I'm really tired. Can we do this some other time?"

"Of course. Emmalyn, I'm not trying to hurt you, and I certainly don't intend to hurt our kid."

"You never intend, but it always seems to happen, doesn't it?"

She went to the front door and opened it. She couldn't make eye contact with him as he walked out without another word.

16 BROTHERS IN ARMS

LUKAS DROVE AWAY FROM Emmalyn's house with his mind whirling at a hundred miles an hour. Emmalyn was right, and it was eating him alive. She and the baby deserved better than what he'd given her the first time around. He wasn't sure how, but he needed to figure out how to answer her and quickly.

He pulled up at his father's house and was happily surprised to find his brother's bright orange muscle car parked in the driveway next to his dad's old Oldsmobile. Lukas shook his head at the old but well-maintained car. Lukas had offered to buy his father a new car many times over the years, but Pop insisted there was nothing wrong with the old car. He grabbed his duffle bag from the passenger seat and made his way to the door.

Using his key, he let himself in the house. As usual, his father and brother were in the middle of a loud, angry argument, though Lukas couldn't quite tell what it was about. He dropped his bag by the door, and shook his head before following the sound of the yelling through the house to the back porch.

"Hey, hey, hey, what the hell are you two fighting about now?" he broke in as he stepped out to the sunroom attached to the back of Pop's house.

"Lukas! What are you doing here?" Pop asked in surprise.

"Hey, bro, nice of you to come visit me," Jaxon smiled.

"Oh, shut up, boy. He ain't here to see your trifling ass!" Pop swiped at Jaxon.

"Nice to know some things never change." He reached down and slapped his dad's shoulder before hugging his brother. It had been over a year since they'd seen one another.

Jaxon, a chemical engineer and commissioned officer in the United States Marine Corps, had been deployed overseas for the past eight months. They didn't know exactly where he'd been sent, but every time something blew up in one of the countries the United States was at war with, he had a feeling Jaxon was behind it. Jaxon and their father had never seen eye to eye on anything. Visits home usually involved some kind of blow up between the two. "How long you home?"

"Two months. Apparently, I like my job too much for comfort. I'm on ordered rest and relaxation."

"Nice."

"Did you bring Sunny with you?" Pop interjected.

"Uh, no, Pop. She stayed in San Diego."

"I like her, bro. She is fine! Yo, she got a sister? A cute cousin or something?"

"Looks aren't everything, Jaxon," Lukas said cryptically.

"The hell they ain't!" Lukas and Jaxon burst into laughter, but their father didn't join in.

"Lukas. What happened? What are you doing in North Carolina?" Pop cut through their laughter.

"Damn, Pop, can't Lukas come into the state without you being grouchy?"

"I'm talking to your brother, not you, so shut your mouth." Pop shook his pointer finger at Jaxon, and the three were transported ten years into the past.

Jaxon's eyes darted in confusion back and forth between his father and brother. "I've missed something here. Pop is always happy when his favorite son is home. Unless... Lukas has messed up. Yes! I am so glad I'm here to witness this one."

Pop rolled his eyes and huffed loudly. "Jaxon, go to your room if you can't behave like a human being. Lukas, start talking."

"Did he just send me to my room? I'm a United States Marine Corps officer. You can't just order me around like a kid."

"Not in this house. I'm the captain of this ship!"

Lukas and Jaxon exchanged looks. "Should I tell him I'm ranked higher than a captain or what?"

"Nah, it won't help."

"God damn it, Lukas!"

Lukas sighed and sat down on one of the loungers. He closed his eyes and spoke, "Sunny left me."

"What? Why?" Pop pushed when Lukas refused to explain further.

"Well, Emmalyn came to San Diego to see me. I wasn't home, but Sunny was." Lukas sighed as he recounted the interaction between the two women. He cringed when he recalled the look on Em's face as she walked out of his house.

"Oh snap! Cat fight."

Lukas gave his brother a dirty look. Jaxon recognized the line and promptly stepped back across it. He knew Emmalyn was still a somewhat sore issue between his brother and father.

"Why the hell is she stalking you clear across the country?" Pop looked like he was about to have a heart attack. His eyes were bulged with anger.

"She wasn't stalking me, Pop. She..." He couldn't say it. He did not want to tell his father that he'd gotten his ex-girlfriend pregnant. But he may as well get it over with. It wasn't the first ass-chewing he'd gotten that day, and it wouldn't be the last. "She's pregnant. She came to California to tell me."

"WHAT?" Jaxon and Pop exclaimed in unison. Lukas didn't bother opening his eyes. He knew the look each was giving just as clearly as if he was looking at them. He cracked an eye when Jaxon began to laugh. All he could do was sigh.

"Pop, I don't need a lecture on this. I'm going to take care of my kid."

"And what about Emmalyn?" Pop demanded.

"She doesn't want me. Hell, if she had her way, I'd go back to California and cease to exist. She didn't know about Sunny."

"Damn, bro, that is fucked up. I know how much you loved her."

It was more than Lukas expected from his brilliant but very immature younger brother. The two brothers were exactly ten months apart. Jaxon and Lukas had been toddlers when their mother committed suicide. They relied on one another for support and always had each other's backs. They were complete opposites but loved each other unconditionally.

"That girl is ruining your life. Mark my words." Angry beyond words, Pop stormed back into the house.

LATER THAT NIGHT, AS they had done countless times while growing up, Jaxon and Lukas snuck out of the house and went down into the woods. They'd had hundreds of talks down near the creek that ran through the woods at the edge of their father's land. The spot was as peaceful as it always was. Their father had fielded several offers to buy the land over the years, but he was content to stay right where he was.

"Pop's wrong. I don't think Emmalyn is going to ruin your life."

"Thanks. I needed to hear that," Lukas admitted, poking the ground with a stick he'd picked up during their walk.

"I think you're ruining your life." Jaxon had always been the academic in the family. Lukas took a while to find his footing and career. Jaxon, on the other hand, had a plan from the start—college then the Marines. He'd wanted to be a military officer since he was a kid, and it was the only thing Jaxon took seriously. Everything else was just a colossal joke.

"How so?"

"Are you sure you and Emmalyn can make it this time? You were a mess when she dumped you the last time."

"I told you, she doesn't want anything to do with me."

"That's complete bullshit, and we both know it, so be honest with me. Or are you still lying to yourself where she's concerned?"

Lukas stared at his brother. Damned if that wasn't exactly what Emmalyn had told him earlier that day.

"I can see from your face that you are, in fact, still very much in denial." Jaxon laughed. His brother's habit of living life by the seat of his pants left no room for introspection. He shook his head and laughed again.

"I had this exact conversation with Emmalyn earlier today. She told me that I wasn't being honest with her. I mean, I thought I was. She said I didn't get. She was right. I don't get it." Lukas tossed the stick toward the water. It made a brief splash before sinking into the creek. He rolled his head on his shoulders, hoping for an epiphany. It didn't come.

Jaxon stared at his brother. He didn't want to get involved in whatever Lukas had going on, but the pure misery on Lukas's face forced Jaxon to step in. "When you and Emmalyn were dating, you put anyone and everyone before her. You loved her, no doubt, but it didn't take much for you to set her aside to help someone else—especially Pop. And you know how Pop feels about Em."

Lukas frowned. "Emmalyn didn't need me to tend her. She's never been that kind of girl."

"You're such a dumbass," Jaxon mocked. "Every woman is that kind of girl. You can't tell people you love them, and then not think enough about them to show up when they need you. So the question is—why would you treat the woman you love that way? Why wouldn't you make her your first priority?"

Understanding began to dawn on Lukas. Jaxon smiled at the look of astonishment on Lukas's face before continuing. "Pop always told us that all we had was each other and that no woman should come between us. I turned that into focusing on my career. So, yeah, I'm busting ass in the Marines, but I go home alone every night. And you took the one person you love more than anything and treated her like some side chick."

"Fuck. I didn't see it." Lukas punched Jaxon in the arm. "Why the fuck didn't you say something before?"

Jaxon laughed hard. "What makes you think I knew that all along? The Marines sent me home because blowing up people and places no longer bothered me. I became a machine. I had to see a therapist. Stupid fucking new Marine Corps. Wanna make sure we aren't all going to shoot up a bunch of civilians or embarrass the Corps somehow. It was with the therapist that I understood all this."

Lukas and Jaxon sat quietly, stewing in their own thoughts. The brothers had been through so much, together and individually. It was nice to be able to just sit and talk again.

"I do love her, you know. I want to be with her and the baby," Lukas said.

"I know. But Emmalyn isn't going to listen to a word you have to say because you've said it all before. If you can't be what you've said you'll be, you should give up now."

"Hell, I'm not even sure that'll work with her."

Lukas and Jaxon sat silent for a minute. Jaxon smiled at Lukas, and Lukas immediately sighed. He knew that look. Jaxon was about to say something stupid. He didn't disappoint.

"So, Sunny's single now? Mind if I look her up?"

17 TRUE CONFESSIONS

LUKAS KNEW HE NEEDED to figure some things out if he was going to fix the mess he and Emmalyn had made of their relationship. One thing he already knew for sure was that he needed to convince Isabel and Zavia that he was serious if he was to have any chance at winning Emmalyn back—or at least for them to be friends enough to be able to co-parent. He'd sent an email to Zavia, Isabel and Emmalyn inviting them to dinner in a couple days at Em's favorite restaurant. He included Brian and Jaxon to ensure he had some non-hostile people there to watch his back.

"Man, are you sure about this? It's kinda like eating with a nest of vipers," Brian asked skeptically. They were sitting in Brian's office going over the plans for the dinner Lukas was hosting. "I mean, I've got your back, but this seems risky."

Lukas was leaning back in the chair opposite Brian's desk, tossing a baseball in the air. "I gotta do something. I've got to go back to San Diego soon, and I don't want to go without trying once more. Just say you're coming. Jaxon is coming too," he added.

Brian rolled his eyes. He loved Jaxon like a brother, but Jaxon had a tendency to make things worse, not better. "Have you told him to behave himself? You know how he gets in serious situations."

"He swears on his Marine uniform that he will act like a gentleman."

On the night of the dinner, Lukas, Brian, and Jaxon arrived at the restaurant a bit early to make sure everything was set up properly. Zavia and her husband, Robert, arrived first. One look at Zavia's furious face and Lukas immediately wanted to run and hide, but he needed Zavia's support. That didn't make him any more comfortable though.

"Zavia, thanks for coming. Robert, good to see you man. This is Brian and my brother Jaxon."

Zavia didn't even bother to hide her annoyance. She walked right up to Lukas and poked him in the chest. "I can't change who the father of Em's baby is, but if you hurt her or that child, I will gut you like a pig. Because there are children around, I won't tell you what I have planned for your genitals."

Robert grabbed her and gently pulled her away. "Zee, give the man a break. He's going to be a father. I doubt he brought us here to cause Em any pain. Right?" Robert gave Lukas a sympathetic but stern look.

"Right," Jaxon interjected. "My brother is very excited about the baby and wants to celebrate."

"Umm hmm. He just better watch himself. I won't let him live long if he hurts my girl again."

Zavia sat down just as Isabel and Emmalyn walked in. Emmalyn looked beautiful. Pregnancy certainly agreed with her. Lukas started to tell her that, but a flash of pain across her face caused him to take pause.

"Emmy, is something wrong?" he asked, rushing to her side. He took her hand and led her toward the table.

She frowned in response. "Why do you ask?"

"Because you look like something hurts." He knew that was the wrong thing to say when she reached up and grabbed his ear, pulling his face even with hers.

"There is a baby inside me that wants to eat its way out like the monster in Alien. Anything else you want to know?"

"No. You're pretty. Please let my ear go." She let him go and turned to say hi to Brian. Her face turned to pure pleasure when she spotted Jaxon.

"Jaxon! I'm so happy to see you. You look wonderful. War agrees with you." She pulled him into a hug and kissed his cheek.

"And pregnancy agrees with you. You look glorious!"

Em patted Jaxon's cheek and hugged him again. "I'm glad one of you Upton boys knows how to talk to pregnant women." She turned and stuck out her tongue at Lukas. He could only shake his head. Jaxon helped her to the chair between him and Lukas.

Everyone seated and orders placed, the conversation went on smoothly. Jaxon told stories of his time overseas that kept everyone laughing. Lukas tried to engage Emmalyn in conversation a couple of times, but Zavia or Isabel interrupted in an effort to keep the peace. Jaxon tried to keep the ladies entertained and give his brother a chance to talk to Em, but they weren't having any part of that.

Finally, Jaxon asked Lukas about his job. "So, bro, what's going on in the world of information technology?"

Brian reached out and snagged the last roll but split it when Em growled at him.

"Well, we've sold our last tool set to a major software company. And with Isabel and Emmalyn's help, we believe our next set of tools will innovate mobile marketing and provide a platform for small businesses. Brian has designed a strategy to launch, and we've hired Isabel and Emmalyn to do the user interface development."

"That must be interesting. Is this something big in San Diego?" Zavia asked pointedly.

FAIRYTALE LOST

"Uh, no, actually we're looking to launch in Charlotte." Lukas kept his eyes focused on his plate as everyone at the table stared at him.

"Here?" Emmalyn choked out. "So, Brian will be leading the launch?"

"Not exactly. He and I are co-chairing the launch. I'll be relocating to Charlotte in the next month to prepare."

Emmalyn was completely speechless. She, Isabel, and Zavia simply stared at Lukas as though he'd grown a second head.

"That's awesome news, Lukas," Jaxon prompted. It hadn't escaped his notice that Emmalyn looked less than pleased by this bit of news.

"Yeah, thanks. I'll be renting a place here before I go back to San Diego at the end of the week to close out a bit of business."

Lukas watched the wave of emotions play across Emmalyn's face. He could tell she wasn't happy about being told in such a public way, but she didn't seem angry. That had to be a good sign, right?

"Well, since it's open season on announcements, I have one as well," Emmalyn said, relying on Jaxon's friendly face for strength. She could feel Lukas's warmth and wanted to both move closer to him and move away. She took a deep breath and said, "I've applied for a transfer to the Charleston office."

The entire table sat in dumbfounded silence. Isabel and Zavia in particular sat gape- mouthed and confused, not sure what to say. Emmalyn took the silence as a blessing and continued speaking. "I think this is going to be best for me and the baby. You know, start over someplace fresh with a slower pace of life."

"Wait, you're leaving Charlotte? You can't be serious," Zavia asked skeptically.

Em took a deep breath and began to explain her side of things. "Zavia, I know you don't agree."

"You're damn right I don't agree. I know things are a bit hectic here, but at least you have me and Isabel. We can be your support system, and the baby's father would be around to help. Babies are a lot of work. Robert and I are still figuring it out, and Jared is old enough to feed and clothe himself now."

"I understand that," Em tried to say, but Zavia wasn't quite finished.

"Clearly, not if you want to move three hours away."

"I've given this a lot of thought, and I've made up my mind. I am well aware that you don't think I can do this, Zavia. You've made that clear on several occasions."

"I never…," she started, but Em cut her off.

"You most certainly have. But this is my life and my baby. Either support my decision or shut the hell up." Em stood up and turned to walk away.

"Where are you going now?" Isabel asked.

"To the bathroom. Or do we need to take a vote on that too?" She didn't wait for an answer and stormed off in the direction of the restrooms.

"Why don't you say something?" Isabel asked, rounding on Lukas. He was obviously still stunned by Em's announcement.

"What should I have said?" he said weakly.

"It's your baby too, damn it. Make her stay here," Isabel hissed.

"Oh yeah, my position in her life is so rock solid I can make her feel like a child like Zavia does," Lukas countered.

Zavia opened then closed her mouth. She knew he was right. She flopped back in her seat heavily. "She's been acting so distant the last few days. I thought it was just the hormones." Zavia took a long sip of her wine. She turned to Lukas and said something she never thought she'd hear herself say.

"You'd better figure something out soon. She's running away from me and from you. If you don't find a way to fix things with her, you're going to lose her, and your baby."

EXACTLY ONE WEEK LATER, Lukas called Emmalyn and asked her to meet him for lunch. She didn't want to go but figured she owed him at least that much. He hadn't spoken a single word to her since her announcement. During the drive to the restaurant, Em practiced her speech about how her moving to Charleston is in everyone's best interest. Assured she'll be able to hold her own, she strode into the restaurant, confident and ready for battle.

Lukas was visibly furious with her. She tried to give him her speech, but he didn't want to hear any of it.

"So, without so much as a word to me, you decide to take my kid to South Carolina. Just like that? I don't get a say," he snarled at her, angry that she would just up and leave like this.

She wasn't sure she'd ever seen Lukas this angry, especially not with her. She put up her hands in defense. "I didn't know you were moving back here. If you were still living in San Diego, what difference would it have made?" This was not going at all like she'd planned. Lukas wasn't supposed to care this much. Was he?

"Tell me something, Emmalyn. If I hadn't come to your office that day and seen your little baby bump, would you have told me about the baby?" Lukas shook with the effort to remain calm. Yelling at a pregnant woman wouldn't win him any points, and it would be the fastest way to get Em to shut down on him completely.

"I went to your house to tell you, but you were planning to marry someone else," she said, her defenses going way up.

He paused but didn't let up. "That doesn't answer my question. But for the record, my marrying Sunny would not have magically made that baby someone else's. That would have still been my child. Would you have told me?" Lukas looked her square in the eye and waited for her to lie to him.

"No, I wouldn't have," she said instead, his surprise visible.

"And now you're trying to keep the baby away from me?" He leaned back in his chair and crossed his arms over his chest.

"No, it's not like that. I want to start over some-where else. Can't you understand that?" Emmalyn didn't know how to make Lukas—or anyone—understand. In her heart, she needed a fresh start and to get away from everything that was causing her stress. This pregnancy was much, much harder on her than she'd let on to anyone. She needed peace to make it through this pregnancy with any sanity, and she knew damn well she'd never be able to have it in Char-lotte.

"No, Emmalyn, I can't. Your friends are here. Eve-ryone you know, with the exception of your mother, is here. Why go to Charleston? What are you running from?" Desperation radiated from his gut to his chest. He had to find a way to convince her to stay.

"Lukas, I can't explain it. It's just something I have to do, something I want to do." She still wasn't ready to come clean about what this pregnancy was doing to her health—both physically and mentally.

"And now that you know I'll be here and want to be a part of the baby's life, will you still leave?"

She looked at him and tried to gauge the situation. The truth was, his moving back to Charlotte made her want to leave even more, but she didn't think admitting that would help the situation very much. But the alternative was lying, and she knew he'd see right through her. "Yes," was all she could say.

Lukas swore long and angrily under his breath, though Em caught each and every word. She honestly didn't think he'd care this much. He never seemed to before.

"We can figure something out, some kind of custody arrangement that will work for both of us. I'm only going a few hours away."

Lukas didn't respond. He just stood up from the table and, without another word, left the restaurant.

18 Uh, Houston...

IN TRUTH, EMMALYN DID not settle into pregnancy very smoothly. She loved working, but since becoming pregnant, she simply didn't have the stamina to push as she did before. As a result, her body was rebelling against her. She was tired all the time and couldn't seem to eat enough to maintain her energy levels. Em struggled to learn how to listen to her body and slow down when she needed to.

She'd just finished unpacking some things she'd bought for the baby and had finally found a comfortable place on the sofa when the doorbell rang. At just eleven weeks pregnant, her legs were beginning to bother her, and wandering the stores for several hours just wasn't a good idea. She lumbered to the door and peeked through the peephole. To her surprise, Lukas was outside, his arms full of bags.

"Lukas, what on earth is all that?" she inquired as she held the door open for him.

He dropped the bags on the floor in the living room, his face full of excitement. "I was in the store, and I saw this stuff. I wasn't sure what you needed, so I bought one of each. I figure we can go through it, and you can tell me what you need and what you don't."

She laughed. "You're ridiculous." She bent down and started looking through the bags, though when she tried to straighten up she grimaced. Lukas noticed.

"What's wrong?" He helped her back to the sofa.

"Nothing," she replied and tried to keep her face neutral. It didn't work. She sighed before fessing up. "I went shopping earlier, and I must have overdone it. My legs and lower back are killing me," she confessed.

He led her over to the sofa and pulled her down beside him. He shifted to the other end of the sofa. "Here let me see your feet." She hesitated a second too long, so he reached down and pulled her swollen feet to his lap. He rubbed and stretched her toes and ankles, making her groan in pleasure.

"I'd tell you to stop," she murmured, "but I really want you to keep going."

"Hold on a sec." Laughing, he pulled his phone out of his pocket with one hand while massaging the ball of one of her feet with the other. He texted Brian and

Jaxon and told them that he wouldn't be joining them for drinks.

"Got a hot date?" Em joked. Eyes closed, a mischievous grin on her face, she laughed out loud when he tickled the bottom of her feet.

"Behave, will you? I was just letting Brian and Jaxon know I wasn't going to make it tonight. Have you eaten recently?" He tried looking her over for an answer, but she was hiding her face from him. Under her eyes was dark with exhaustion and her skin looked pale.

"I had something earlier. I'm a bit hungry. I'll cook myself something. You go on ahead and meet your brother and Brian. I'll be okay." She paused for a moment before asking, "Does this mean you're not still angry with me for moving?"

He shook his head and tsked her. "I'm not leaving you. How about Chinese food? I know you have menus," he laughed. He simply ignored her last question, instead focusing on this time. He wanted to show her they could get along, and then she'd know she didn't need to leave. Up first, though, was feeding her. Something was off about her coloring, and it concerned him, though he decided not to ask her anything specific.

She pouted when he gently laid her feet on the sofa and went in search of the menus. He found her folder of delivery menus right where she'd told them they'd be in the kitchen, then he called in the order. In the meantime he walked her through the stuff he'd bought earlier. They shared a few laughs as Lukas showed her all the clothes and things that he'd bought but that the baby wouldn't be able to wear for a quite some time.

"How was I supposed to know they come in different sizes," asked Lukas, confused and grumpy that Em was laughing at him.

"Um, the tag on the inside. Just like in your clothes, silly man. These clothes won't fit until the baby is six-to-nine months." She held out the tag for him to look at. "See. Six-to-nine months."

"Should I take it back? Get smaller stuff?"

"I don't suppose so. I mean, the baby will grow into it. I've bought a bunch of newborn and three-to-six month stuff. If you look in the spare room at the end of the hall upstairs, you'll see the bags. Grab them, and I'll show you what I have."

Lukas trotted off upstairs, returning quickly with the bags of stuff Emmalyn bought earlier that day during her shopping trip.

"Jesus, Emmalyn, is there anything left in the store?" he joked.

"You're one to talk." Emmalyn swung her feet to the floor and slowly slid to the floor from where she sat on the sofa. She pulled things out of the bags, holding them up for Lukas to see then folding them back up neatly.

"You bought everything in yellow and green. You don't know yet if it's a girl or a boy?"

"Not yet. The appointment for that is in a couple weeks. If you want to come, you can, you know," Emmalyn offered quietly. She raised her eyes and met Lukas's shit-eating grin.

"Of course I want to come. I bet the baby looks like me," he boasted.

She laughed and rolled her eyes. "Oh Lord. Shut up, and open the door. The food is here."

Emmalyn and Lukas spent an entertaining evening eating cheap Chinese food and watching B-movies on one of the science fiction channels. She fell asleep before the end of the first movie. Lukas woke her up and, after a number of foul words and growls, convinced her to go to bed.

THE NEXT MORNING, LUKAS woke Emmalyn up with a full breakfast, served to her in bed. Eggs, sausage, toast, fruit, and juice—none of which had existed in Emmalyn's refrigerator before—were laying on the bed beside her.

"Your refrigerator is a disgrace to adulthood, Emmalyn," Lukas complained. "There is something in there that has more hair on it than I have. What in the hell have you been eating?" Lukas shook his head then sat on the cushioned bench at the foot of her bed.

"Lukas, what the hell are you doing in my house?" she squeaked in surprise.

"Making sure you have a proper breakfast for once. Did you know that you don't even have oatmeal in your pantry? Just something called quinoa. Is that really a thing? I've never heard of it." He shifted a bit and rubbed her leg through the covers.

She pulled the covers over her head, disturbing the tray of food but not knocking anything over. "Lukas, I swear to God if you don't stop all that damn chatter, I'm going to murder you," she groaned.

"I'll stop talking when you start eating," he replied sweetly.

She gave him a very dirty look before hoisting herself upright, pulling the tray onto her lap. She grabbed a piece of toast and took a bite. She was much hungrier than she'd thought. Lukas watched her eat all the food on the tray then cleared the dishes. Emmalyn heard the water running downstairs in the kitchen. She shuffled down the hall then down a flight of stairs to find Lukas hand-washing the plates and pans from breakfast.

"I have two questions for you, and you'd better answer them correctly. One, how did I get into my pajamas? And two, where did all this food come from?"

Lukas dried his hands and turned to face Emmalyn. She was adorable with her new belly poking out of her nightshirt. Her hair was a tangled mess that had started out in a loose bun on the top of her head but had gone amuck during the night. "Well, I took your clothes off and put you in your nightshirt. Then, since you were dead to the world, I went to the grocery store and bought you a refrigerator's worth of food."

"I see," was all Em said as she sat at the bistro table in her kitchen.

"You might want to think about hiring some help, Emmalyn. This may be more than you can handle."

"So, what? You don't want to be my nanny anymore?"

He laughed and sat down across from her. "I already have a full-time job, though I don't mind helping you out."

It was Emmalyn's turn to laugh. Lukas's face went solemn. Emmalyn realized her mistake, but she knew she was right. Lukas's history of reliability didn't stand up to scrutiny, though she had to admit he was trying. She stood up, walked around the table, and gently sat on Lukas's lap. She gave him a quick kiss on the lips. Leaning in to him, forehead to forehead, she smiled at him as she looked into his eyes.

"I appreciate your help, Lukas. I really do. Thank you for taking care of me. Zee's right. I'm a disaster."

"I know I'm not always on time or around when you need me, but I'm trying, I swear."

"I know."

He smacked her lightly on her butt, signaling that he needed to get up. "I need to run home and change before work. And you need to get moving, or you're going to be late."

She stood up, and he followed suit. He pulled her into a hug and held her, just held her for a minute. She'd always felt so right in his arms, and now was no different. He kissed her lightly on the top of her head and turned toward the door.

"I'll text you the info for the doctor's appointment. Make sure you write it down, and don't be late," she called.

"I won't. I'll come back later tonight and check on you. I'm heading back to San Diego tomorrow for a couple of days to clear up some business, but then I'm coming back here for good." She smiled at him, and his gut tightened. He needed to leave before he found himself unable to. "I'll see you later, Emmalyn."

19 TNT

"EMMALYN, YOU NEED TO go. You're going to be late for your appointment." Isabel fussed and frowned. She'd known Em was going to do this.

"I'm almost done. I just need to back the files up to the server before I shut down. It's not as if they can start without me, you know."

"Damn it, Emmalyn, you are infuriating!" Isabel slammed shut her laptop and stomped over to Emmalyn's desk. As usual, it was a disaster of papers, books, and sticky notes. Isabel took it all in and wondered what kind of genius Em was to be able to function in such confusion. "Are you scared? Do you want me to go with you?"

Emmalyn laughed, never taking her eyes off the screen. Two more clicks of her mouse, and she was finished with her task. Finally, she shut her laptop. "See. All done. And no, you don't have to do that. Lukas is meeting me there."

Isabel and Emmalyn were interrupted by their boss. Meanie Martin was a tall skinny man with thinning, mousy-brown hair and pasty-white skin that hadn't seen sun in ages. He considered himself a ladies man, though none of the women he dated would have been considered a lady by any stretch of the imagination. "Emmalyn, good, you're still here. Charleston has accepted your request to transfer. If you agree to the new terms, you are to report there once you've completed your maternity leave. Congrats on the new bundle of joy. Good thing you don't sleep much."

His creepy laugh could be heard as he walked down the hall away from their office.

"Seriously," Isabel asked, totally creeped out. "What a dick!"

"I know. But I can't worry about that weirdo at the moment. Gotta get to my ultrasound." Emmalyn smiled brightly. She was so excited to finally learn her baby's gender.

"Just remember, if it's a girl, you have to name her after me," Isabel called to her.

"Of course. And just so you know, Zavia made me make the same promise to her, and I have no intention of following through on either request."

"HE'S COMING. I THINK. I mean, he said he'd be here." Emmalyn looked at her watch and contemplated calling Lukas again. She had tried to call him on her way to the doctor's office to remind him, but his phone had gone to voicemail. He was late, but she knew he'd be there. They had just discussed the appointment a couple of days ago. Emmalyn smiled lamely at the nurse, who was clearly trying to get this appointment over with.

"Do you have any questions we can cover before your husband arrives?" The nurse was adjusting the machinery so that when Lukas arrived, all she'd have to do was fire everything up.

"No." She paused. He was fifteen minutes late. She sighed deeply. "Just go ahead. I'll tell him what he needs to know later."

"I can record the ultrasound and put it on a DVD if you like," the nurse offered sadly, slightly guilty at rushing the sad woman on the table.

Emmalyn couldn't smile, so she said, "Okay, thanks."

The nurse gave her a pitying look before switching everything on. Emmalyn closed her eyes and listened to what the nurse was telling her, and nothing she did could stop her tears from falling.

"HEY, MAN, IS THAT the door?" Jaxon was battling for his life, this marathon game of Halo was now entering its fifth hour. Brian and Lukas were so focused on the game that they couldn't hear whomever it was knocking loudly.

"Damn it, come in," Lukas bellowed, his eyes never leaving the screen as hundreds of zombie-like creatures swarmed their little team.

"What in the entire fuck do you think you're doing?" Emmalyn's voice was rough from having cried on the drive across town. Her eye makeup had run, and she looked a frightful mess.

The game carried on as the three men turned to face the exceptionally angry pregnant woman standing nearby.

"Emmy, what are you doing here, baby? You get off early today or something?" Lukas dropped the controller and walked slowly around the sofa, approaching Emmalyn like a trapped animal. "You look pretty."

She narrowed her eyes at him as a half dozen ways to end his life flipped through her brain like a Rolodex. "Lukas, what day is this?" she ground out through gritted teeth.

He gave her a lopsided smile. "I'll go out on a limb and say Thursday."

She didn't smile. Her eyes welled up, and her throat threatened to release yet another sob. "Are you going to stand there grinning at me like a goddamn idiot? You missed the ultrasound appointment! Playing video games. You don't even have a good reason this time."

His eyes went wide with fear and confusion. "Oh no. That appointment isn't until tomorrow. You said the twenty-fifth."

Em walked over to him and slapped him across the back of his head. "Lukas, you horse's ass, it is the twenty-fifth."

"Jesus, Emmy, it was just one doctor's appointment; you'll have others. Why are you getting so bent out of shape?" He wracked his brain for possible reasons for her going off the deep end like this and came back with nothing. He turned and walked back to the sofa, having concluded that Em was hormonally overreacting and his game needed his attention.

Emmalyn could feel the tears about to start up again and turned to dash out of the house. Lukas stared at her back as she left the apartment. He couldn't move until he heard the door slam.

THE TEARS FLOWED IN streams as Emmalyn rushed down the stairs and out of the building.

"Young lady," came a concerned voice. "What's wrong, Emmalyn?"

Lukas's dad reached for her, and she pulled away. She knew he didn't like her and didn't want him seeing her in this state.

"Nothing. I'm fine," she muttered, sniffling loudly.

"Clearly, that's not true. What has my idiot son done now?"

She shook her head. Let Lukas explain his actions to his own father. She just wanted to get away from there.

"Ask him," she spat out. She reached in her bag and pulled out the DVD of the ultrasound. Pop looked at it then back at her. "Tell Lukas I've accepted the job in Charleston."

She didn't wait for him to respond. She rushed over to her car and fought with the handle. Of course, she wouldn't be able to get the damn thing to work.

"I'm getting a new car tomorrow," she thought to herself.

Pop had followed her out to the parking lot. "He loves you," he cut through her frustrated thoughts, "you know, always has. No matter how much I tried to tell him it wasn't a good idea, he still loved you. If you leave, it'll break his heart." Pop reached out and touched Em's arm, hoping that she'd look at him. When she did, he wished he hadn't said anything at all. Her eyes were glassy with unshed tears. He could see what Lukas saw in her, and it broke his heart.

"What's the point in loving people if you can't rely on them? If they aren't there when you need them? If I have to do this by myself, then I may as well be by myself."

The lock on the car popped, and she got in as fast as her growing belly would allow. Emmalyn gave Pop a last sad smile then drove off.

Pop walked into Lukas's new apartment and found the house under attack. Lukas was furiously throwing boxes around, yelling.

"Fucking Christ, I forget one little thing, and she just goes off. I can't read her. I mean, what is her deal?"

Finally finding what he was looking for, he booted up his tablet and tried to get the calendar to open.

"Lukas, she's gone." He handed Lukas the DVD. "She's taking the job in Charleston."

"But ... she said she wasn't. She said she was going to stay here." Lukas ran around looking for his keys and phone. "I'm going to talk to her. She can't take my kid away from me."

"Kids," Pop corrected. "Take a look at that disc. And I wouldn't recommend going after her. She's in no fit state to talk to you right now, not to mention, all this stress can't be good for the babies.

Lukas stared dumbly at the disc. "Shit," he whispered.

Brian walked over and took the disc from him. "I'll put it in the player, man."

Lukas and Pop followed Brian to the living room. Brian handed the cover back to Lukas and sat down. The screen blinked on, and the sound of the baby's heartbeat could be heard before the picture came on.

"Sounds like the heartbeat has an echo or a heart murmur," Jaxon mumbled, sounding confused.

"It's twins. She's carrying twins." Lukas passed the disc cover over to Jaxon, who promptly swore under his breath. The picture flickered on, and the faint outline of the first baby could be seen. The picture shifted somewhat, and there, to the left of the first pair of legs, another leg. Then a second head could be seen. "Shit. I missed finding out the sex of the babies."

"How did you miss this?" Pop asked angrily.

"I forgot. I figured it was just another appointment. She has so many. I didn't think it would matter." Lukas paused and watched the screen again. It had stopped moving, and the scene was frozen, the camera seeming to hover over the babies' heads. The disc cover had said baby girl A Chase and baby girl B Chase. Girls. He and Emmalyn were having twin girls. Lukas's body went limp as the realization of what he'd really missed washed over him. He felt like the horse's ass Em had called him earlier.

He understood now—all of it. She had every right to be angry with him. He needed to find her and apologize. Lukas jumped up, keys in hand, phone still missing.

"I gotta go talk to her," he said, frantically looking for his phone. He was going to call her and find out where she was and get there as fast as humanly possible.

"And say what, man? Sorry I missed out on seeing our babies for the first time because I was in the middle of a Halo firefight with my boys?" Incredulous, Jaxon was equal parts furious with and sympathetic toward his brother.

Lukas wracked his brain for something, anything, that would fix the mess he'd caused. He and Em were finally getting to a place where she wasn't so guarded with him. Now none of that was going to matter. She'd go back to shutting him out, and he'd go back to watching from the sideline.

"I have to tell her I love her, that I'm sorry, that…," Lukas didn't know what else to say. He had to think of something and fast. He loved Emmalyn with all his heart and wanted to be with her and the babies. "I can't lose her again. There has to be something I can say or do to win her heart back."

His father walked over and stood directly in front of him. He put his hands on Lukas's shoulders and looked him squarely in the eyes. Lukas steeled himself for another lecture on how Emmalyn wasn't good enough for him.

"The woman I saw just now outside this building is so much in love with you she can't see straight, no doubt about that. But she's hurt, and she's scared.

You don't need to win her heart because her heart is already yours. You need to figure out a way to convince her brain that you aren't going to keep letting her down."

Lukas laughed sadly. "All I ever do is let her down." He fell back against the wall, lost. He looked at Brian and Jaxon for something, anything, but they were just as lost as he was.

"Then maybe you need to figure that out before you go chasing after her."

Lukas slunk back down, perplexed about what he should do. He knew his father was right. A pain grew in his chest as he realized he had absolutely no idea how to make it happen.

20 Mea Culpa. Mostly.

LUKAS SAT PARKED OUTSIDE Emmalyn's house
for a good ten minutes trying to work up the nerve to
go in and talk to her. He'd spotted Zavia and Isabel's
cars in the driveway and had had second then third
thoughts about what he wanted to say. He was about
to drive away when the memory of the babies' heart-
beats came back to him, steeling his resolve to see this
through. His carelessness had created this mess, and he
needed to make sure he tried to fix it.

He got out of his car and slowly walked up the
drive, practicing exactly what he wanted to say. As he
reached the stoop, he found the door slightly ajar, and
the sound of music playing in one of the upstairs rooms

could be heard. Then he heard Emmalyn's tone-deaf singing and knew she was okay inside.

Knocking loudly and hoping not to startle anyone, he opened the screen door, stuck his head in, and yelled a hello. The music cut off abruptly, and repeated the word in a lower, friendlier tone.

"Lukas?" Zavia was the first to reach him, and her tone was decidedly less friendly. "Get your busted ass out of this house this instant. I warned you...," Zavia stopped talking as Emmalyn came around the corner.

She gave him a half-smile. "Lukas, I'm glad you're here. We need to talk. Guys, please. Give us a minute."

She took his hand and pulled him through the first-floor den and out to the back porch.

"Emmalyn, look, I'm sorry I screwed up again."

Emmalyn waved him off and smiled, though it didn't quite reach her eyes. "I'm sorry I reacted that way. We'll say it was the pregnancy hormones causing me to be so bitchy."

He eyed her suspiciously. She'd never apologized for overreacting, especially when he was clearly at fault. He looked around the yard and noticed all the patio furniture had been wrapped and stacked as if waiting to be taken away. The pain in his chest that had started a few days ago came back full force. "I guess you've accepted the position in Charleston. I thought you weren't leaving until after the babies came."

"I found a renter for my house, so I asked if I could go earlier."

"Em...," Lukas started, but words failed him.

"Lukas, this is how it needs to be. I'm not going to deny you access to your kids, and I will do everything in my power to make sure they know you and spend time with you. But I won't make it through this pregnancy with all the drama that goes on between us. The doctor wants me to remain stress free and focus on staying healthy. We both know I'll never do that here. It's too late for us."

She held up her hand when he opened his mouth to argue with her, but it was the sadness and resignation in her eyes that truly stopped him from speaking up. He closed his eyes and leaned back on the house and didn't open them until he heard the sliding glass door close behind her.

Desperate now to get away, he tried to go through the gate, but it was locked, and he didn't know how to open it. His only option was to go through the house. Without making eye contact with Isabel or Zavia, he rushed through the house and out the front door. He didn't look back before getting in his car and driving away.

Emmalyn watched from an upstairs window as Lukas's car sped off. She crumbled to the bed, tears streaming over her cheeks. Unable to stand it any longer, she lay down on her bed and cried.

Zavia and Isabel hovered just outside the door, unsure whether they should go in or not. Zavia cracked first and went in, sitting beside Em and pulling her into an embrace. Isabel followed, stroking Emmalyn's hair.

"He left me," Em said between sobs. "He just walked out."

Isabel and Zavia exchanged confused looks. Zavia shrugged her shoulders and went back to rubbing Em's back.

"But, sweetie, you said that was what you wanted," pointed out Isabel, gently.

"He didn't even argue. Shouldn't he have at least argued a little bit?" Em sounded pathetic, and she hated Lukas for it.

Both Zavia and Isabel fully understood why Emmalyn was upset, and though neither of them said anything, they were happy he didn't argue. This pregnancy was affecting Emmalyn's health, and she'd been so wrapped up in Lukas and his issues that she wasn't taking care of herself. She hadn't been putting on weight like she was supposed to, and the doctor was far more worried than Em had let on to Lukas. She'd finally told her friends about the issues she was having and the real reason she needed to get out of Charlotte. Emmalyn had developed gestational diabetes, and the resulting fatigue was causing stress on her organs. Zavia could see how everything was wearing on Emmalyn, and though she'd miss her best friend fiercely, she agreed that leaving was the best thing for her.

LUKAS RUSHED AROUND HIS apartment like a mad man. In the two week's since Emmalyn had left Charlotte, he'd spent all his spare time preparing to go after her. His father, brother, and best friend were less than supportive, but he didn't care. His whole life had just moved to Charleston, and nothing and no one was going to keep him from following.

After the sale of his and Brian's online marketing toolset to GlobeComm, he didn't need to worry about money. He worked with Brian to divide up their work for their next mobile launch. With Charleston and Charlotte only three hours apart, he didn't think it would be a big issue. He'd gotten an apartment not too far from where Emmalyn was staying despite his brother's repeated accusations of stalkerish behavior. He didn't care. He just wanted to be near his kids— and the woman he loved.

He walked through the apartment, checking items off his mental list, then began packing things in his car. Jaxon and Brian arrived to help just as he started moving the bigger boxes into the moving trailer he'd rented.

"Jesus, Lukas. You could have waited," Jaxon laughed. "You sure are anxious to get rejected."

Lukas gave his brother a look that said "don't start this again." Jaxon held up his hands in surrender and helped his brother with the box he was carrying.

The three worked in silence, getting as much as they could into the trailer. It was a tight fit, and a lot of things were left for the big moving truck that was coming the next day.

Brian and Jaxon sat on the sofa, having pulled the last of the cold beers out of the sparse refrigerator. Lukas grabbed the one held out by Jaxon and sat down next to them.

"Remind me again why you couldn't just have the movers do all this when they got here?" Brian took a long drink and leaned his head back on the sofa. Lukas had no idea how to pack a box, he thought to himself. "Your boxes are crazy heavy," he whined.

"Yeah, I guess I put too much in there, but I thought that would take up less space."

"Hmm," Jaxon mused. "You guessed wrong."

They were in the midst of a good laugh when Pop walked in. He took in the empty apartment and shook his head in disgust.

"So, you're going through with this ridiculous plan of yours," he growled angrily.

"Pop, I refuse to have this conversation with you again."

"And what am I supposed to do? Your brother has to report back to the base in a couple of weeks."

"You are not helpless. You'll be fine. You were fine while I was in San Diego," Lukas pointed out.

His father opened his mouth to disagree, but his son was right. And he was tired, tired of arguing, tired of worrying. He understood that Lukas was completely dedicated to being there for his kids, but he was an old man. Selfish as it sounded, he enjoyed having someone around to help him.

"Just tell me why you are chasing after someone who clearly doesn't want you? She left you even after you apologized. Why put yourself through that kind of pain?"

Lukas put his beer down and walked over to his father. They'd gone around and around about this over the past two weeks. His father knew perfectly well why he was going. Lukas couldn't understand why his father didn't see the need for him to go after his kids, to be there for them and for the woman who was carrying them.

"I need you to really listen because we are never, ever, having this discussion again. I'm going to be where my kids are. So, Emmalyn could move a thousand times, and that's how many times I would go. She didn't get herself into this by herself and I'll be damned if she's go through this alone. She may never forgive me, and I'll learn to live with that, but that doesn't mean I won't be there for her as a friend, that

I won't be there for the twins when they are born and before."

"Lukas, I never took you for a fool." He tried to walk around Lukas and go further into the room but Lukas blocked him.

"I love her. I have always loved her. And if wanting to make a life with the woman I love and our children makes me a fool, then that's what I'll be. Every. Day."

Lukas stormed out of the apartment, slamming the door behind him. Jaxon and Brian watched him go, but his father couldn't bear to accept that his son was just about lost to him.

Jaxon sensed exactly what his father was thinking. And as he always did, he paid little heed to good sense and said exactly what was on his mind. "You're wrong, Pop. Lukas isn't a fool. He's doing what he needs to do to keep his family together."

"And what do you think I'm trying to do?" he snapped. "I'm trying to keep your brother from getting his heart torn to shreds."

"Emmalyn isn't mom. The sooner you accept that, the less likely it will be that you'll be barred from seeing your granddaughters."

Jaxon frowned at his father before following his brother outside.

21 STORM'S A-BREWING

THE HURRICANE HIT ABOUT two weeks after Emmalyn's arrival in Charleston. With the new job, new team, and new town, Em didn't have much un- packed and was completely exhausted. Luckily for her, it was a Friday night, and since Zee and Isabel were in Charlotte, she didn't have anyone to keep her up late. She'd snuggled into the sofa as the wind tossed the trees in the swamp near her apartment around like twigs. One of the grocery store cashiers who had lived in the area her whole life had assured Em that the storm would be mostly bluster—wind and rain, but not too much in the way of flooding. Emmalyn watched the buckets of waterfall from the sky and wondered if old Peggy might have been wrong about this one. She had just decided to start a new movie when there was a heavy knock on the door.

"I hope they aren't evacuating," she thought to herself as she waddled over to the door. She reached up on tiptoe and looked through the peephole. Sure enough, a police officer was standing outside of her door. She asked him to wait a minute while she grabbed a robe and her raincoat and pulled a pair of sneakers out of the closet.

Grabbing her purse last, she opened the door, not really paying much attention to the man at the door.

She struggled to get her shoes on and announced, "I'll just be a minute, officer. I didn't think there was supposed to be flooding."

"Ma'am, there is no flooding. Um, do you mind coming back to the door?" he asked with uncertainty.

She had on one shoe, and her robe was buttoned incorrectly when she made it back to the door. The policeman stood there looking confused.

"Oh, I'm sorry. What's this all about?" Em asked. There was a man behind the officer, but she couldn't see his face under all the layers of plastic.

"I found this gentleman walking down the off-ramp, and he claims to know you. The storm is whipping up something fierce and will only get worse as the night wears on."

"Oh,...," Emmalyn's voice fell off as Lukas pulled the three layers of hood off and gave her a lopsided and apologetic smile.

"Hi, Em. I hope you don't mind me dropping in like this," he said jokingly.

"Lukas, what the hell are you doing out in all this? It's dangerous out there!" She couldn't focus on anything else. The man was insane.

The cop could sense an argument brewing and didn't want to wait around for the conclusion. "Ma'am, do you know him or not? He really shouldn't be out on the streets in the hurricane."

Emmalyn rolled her eyes and huffed. "Yeah, I know him. He can ride the storm out with me."

"Fine," the cop said testily. "Be safe." He tipped his hat to Emmalyn and scowled at Lukas before he walked off.

"I'm sorry, Emmalyn." He took a step towards the doorway, but Emmalyn's growing tummy blocked his path.

"You are not tracking all that water into my apartment. Wait here."

The door slammed in Lukas's face. A few seconds later, Emmalyn returned with a laundry basket. She held it out to him and said, "Strip."

He started to laugh, but there was no amusement in Emmalyn's face. "I can't strip on your porch. What will your neighbors say?"

"My neighbors will want to know what kind of jackass is out walking down I-526 in a hurricane and not be surprised that said jackass is now taking his wet clothes off before coming in the house." She wagged her eyebrows at him in an effort to get him moving.

Reluctantly, he began to peel off the layers he'd put on before beginning this trek. He had thought he'd be able to beat the rain here, but the weather forecasters in Charleston were just as useless as the ones in Charlotte. Then his truck had nothing better to do than to die on him just as he was getting off the ramp.

To be honest, he wasn't sure what he was going to do anyway. He didn't think the rental office would be open, and he hadn't been able to find a hotel to stay in. He sighed as he pulled his sopping wet sweatpants off and dropped them into the basket.

"Emmy, please don't make me take anything else off. I promise to do anything you ask if you let me keep my wet drawers on."

Emmalyn fought a laugh as she stood to one side to allow him entry into the apartment. "I'm sure I have some of your sweatpants around here somewhere. Let me go look."

She walked into one of the bedrooms and lost the battle with her laughter. She sat on the edge the bed and had herself one the best laughs she'd had in ages. When she could focus her eyes, she found Lukas standing in the doorway staring daggers at her. She should have been able to control herself better, but the look on his face only made her laugh even harder.

"Could you point to the box I should start looking in? I'm getting cold."

That caused Emmalyn to start laughing even harder. She was lost. He sighed and started opening the boxes labeled clothes. In the second box he searched through, he found a pair of sweatpants and a t-shirt of his that he thought he'd lost years ago. He went into the bathroom to take the wet underwear off and put on the dry clothes.

Emmalyn stopped laughing enough to follow him into the bathroom. "Do they fit?"

"I don't remember giving you this shirt. It was one of my favorites," he said shortly.

His eyes rolled when her face turned red from the effort to control her laughing.

"I'm so sorry, Lukas, I don't know what's wrong with me?"

He took a good look at her face. She didn't look any better than she had the last time he'd seen her in Charlotte. She still had bags under her eyes, and her skin still looked like Play-Doh. He'd bet she was exhausted and that was a big contributor to her punch-drunkenness.

"Have you been sleeping?"

That sobered her up. She was not about to get lectured by him. "I've been busy getting settled," she defended.

He followed her down the hall. There was a room with big boxes, many with pictures of baby nursery items on them. He did a quick mental calculation. She had to be a bit over four months pregnant now. He smiled to himself. Just like his super organized, uber-prepared Emmy, he thought to himself. She hated not being prepared or not having a plan. She'd have everything a baby would need well before the babies were scheduled to appear.

She finished the tour back in the living room.

"What movie are you watching?" he asked as the lights flickered and then went completely out. "Never mind."

Emmalyn was prepared despite what the people at the store said. She slowly felt her way to the kitchen and switched on the camping lamp she'd bought. She used that to find the flashlights she had strategically placed throughout the apartment. She grabbed the bigger of them and handed it to Lukas.

She shined the lamp on her arm. It was only six thirty, way too early to go to bed, though she thought she'd be able to fall asleep and stay asleep if she really tried. Emmalyn sighed heavily and moved to the sofa.

The blinds were still up. Watching the storm through the trees surrounding the swamp, Emmalyn was calmed by the crazy winds and rain. She'd always loved storms. Whereas most kids would cower and hide at the booming sound of a thunder clap or the blinding flash of lightning, Em loved it and couldn't get enough. She found comfort in the violence of the storm, loved the smell of the air the next day. It was like the earth was able to reset after the temper tantrum of the storm.

Lukas sat next to her on the sofa, watching her watch the storm. He remembered how much she loved storms, although he didn't think a category 2 hurricane should be worshiped and adored the way Em did. He was deep in his own thoughts when she finally spoke.

"What are you doing here, Lukas? I told you I wanted to start over fresh."

"And I agree. We need to start over fresh." He cut her off when she tried to argue with him. "Emmalyn, it's no secret that I love you more than my life. And it's no secret that I've been a raging idiot when it comes to our relationship—and our friendship. I don't intend to ask for forgiveness. You may be right. Things may well be done between us. But I want to be a father to the baby girls you're carrying, and I'll follow you anywhere to be with them."

"Lukas...," she broke off, feeling the sting of tear behind her eyes.

"Emmalyn, I'm going to be the girls' father no matter what happens between us. I got my own apartment. I won't get in the way of your life. I owe you that much. But I'm asking you to please let me be there to watch my girls grow up."

Emmalyn watched his eyes shine from unshed tears. She couldn't deny him this, but she would make sure he understood the rules before they went any further. She grabbed his ear and yanked. Hard. "You break my babies' hearts, and I will tear you limb from limb," she said in a voice that left no question that she was not joking.

"That sounds fair," was all he could say, not trusting the feral look in her eyes this time.

22   REIGNITING A SPARK

OVER THE NEXT SEVERAL weeks, Emmalyn and Lukas settled into an amiable friendship. His apartment was around the corner from hers, so he was close enough to call, but they weren't in each other's way. The separation from their life in Charlotte was exactly what they needed to rebuild the relationship, not that relearning how to relate to one another was smooth sailing.

Emmalyn had grown accustomed to doing everything for herself. More than once, Lukas had caught her doing more than she should, and he'd fuss. Then she'd fuss. It was a vicious cycle.

It all came to a head one day when he showed up early to put together some furniture for the babies.

Emmalyn was about six-and-a-half months pregnant and was having trouble with shoes with laces, so it never occurred to Lukas that she might have tried to do this on her own.

She opened the door in a huff, wondering why someone was at he door at eight o'clock in the morning.

Lukas stood on the other side holding exactly eight ounces of coffee, since at her last check-up, that was what the doctor said she was allowed to have. He didn't say a word, merely handed the cup to her and waited to be granted entrance.

"I appreciate the caffeine, but why are you here so early? I didn't think you knew what eight a.m. was."

She stepped aside and let him in. She noticed his frown and followed his eyes to the boxes stacked up beside the counter waiting to be taken down to the dumpster.

"Well, I thought I was putting baby furniture together today, but I guess not."

She saw the hurt in his eyes, and it raised her hackles. "I didn't think you were actually going to be here this early, and I didn't feel like waiting until noon for you to show up."

"But I'm here. On time. The time you told me to be here." Understanding hit him like a sucker punch to the gut. "But since I never show up when I say I will, why would you think I would now? Got it."

He turned to leave. He paused with his hand on the doorknob when her hand touched his shoulder.

"Lukas, I know you're trying."

"Well, you know, no man wants to be torn apart limb from limb." He turned to her and tried to smile, but the light had gone out of his eyes.

Emmalyn worked her mind for something, anything she could ask him to do. She hated that she was the reason for the sadness creased on his forehead.

"I got the basic structures together, but I don't have the hand strength to tighten stuff. Do you mind checking them? I'll start sorting all the stuff in bags so we can put them away."

She turned and walked back toward the room that would be the babies'. She went through her mental list of everything she wanted to get done before she wasn't able to move anymore. These were going to be some really big babies, judging from how they were growing. The doctor warned her to expect to be on bed rest for her last month of pregnancy. That was going to be hard.

"I also need the racks in the closet adjusted. I bought some additional ones so we can hang the babies' clothes up. Their stuff is small so, you know." She turned and looked at him, a devilish grin on her face. "You have a lot to get done this weekend. Don't just stand there." She disappeared around the corner, and he quickly followed her.

She worked his muscles from dawn to dusk that weekend and for several weekends after. Lukas was beginning to regret having said anything to Emmalyn about helping with baby stuff.

"She's supposed to get tired," he thought to himself. "Where does she get all this energy?" But with him doing all the heavy lifting and her sitting in her rocker (that he'd put together for her), she wasn't really expending that much energy.

Despite hammering his thumb—twice, splitting several pieces of wood, requiring at least four trips to the hardware store, and drilling the end off of his shoe, he was the happiest he'd been in ages.

Lukas knew he was getting to Emmalyn. She no longer shied away when he tried to touch her and, every so often, allowed herself to be cuddled while they watched TV after dinner. Emmalyn was a terrible cook, so Lukas started making dinners and bringing them to her. After a couple of days, she declared the situation ridiculous and started showing up at his door at six thirty with the expectation of being fed.

He still wanted to be able to kiss her, make love with her. But he was wary of pushing her too far to fast, so he bided his time, intent on making things as easy for her as possible.

He hung up the last pink dress in the last bag from her most recent shopping trip and sighed. He turned to go to find Emmalyn and have her inspect his work once again—he'd learned that asking for an inspection was much better than having one thrust upon him—and found her standing in the doorway, a beer in her hand. She was giving him a strange smile, one he hadn't seen in many years.

Taking the beer and a very long drink, he bent down to kiss her cheek in thanks. At the last second, she shifted her head, and his mouth landed right on hers. Surprised, he tried to pull away to apologize, but she'd wound her arms around his neck and held him in place. He groped around for somewhere to set the can then wrapped his arms around her waist, careful not to pull her too tightly.

She kissed him almost desperately then, remembering where they were, she pulled away. He gave her an arrogant smile, and she punched his shoulder.

"Will you kiss me like that every time I submit to being your house slave from now on?"

"Seeing you among all the baby stuff got me all tingly with emotion. Come on, dinner's ready."

She laughed when he blanched. "Don't worry, I didn't cook. I brought some food back from my last trip to the store, and after dinner, I have some stuff I need you to bring up from the car."

"Jesus, Emmalyn, how many outfits can two baby girls need?" he asked, exasperated.

"Don't worry. I used the credit card you gave me for the hardware store. I still have plenty of money."

"That's really not what I meant," he deadpanned as he sat at the counter.

She fixed him a plate with food overflowing but took only vegetables for herself.

"Get some meat, Emmy. You need the protein," he ordered.

She turned to argue with him but held her tongue when she saw how worried he really was.

"I can't. My stomach's been acting funny, almost like the morning sickness is back. I'll eat these then I'll have some chicken when my stomach settles." She settled herself on a stool next to Lukas but couldn't get comfortable. "I swear my ass doubles in size every week. I'm going to sit on the sofa and eat."

Lukas tried his damnedest not to laugh, but it was a losing battle. He threw his head back and laughed a full belly laugh until, that is, a full piece of broccoli hit him on the back of his head. He turned to look at Emmalyn and saw the tears in her eyes.

He dropped his fork and rushed over to the sofa. He put Emmalyn's plate on the coffee table and pulled her onto his lap. He felt exactly like the horse's ass she was always calling him.

"I am so sorry, sweetheart. Please, please, please don't cry. You're pretty, and I love your butt, no matter what size you think it is." Lukas kissed her on the head and rocked her like a child. She tolerated it for exactly seventeen seconds before her tears turned to anger.

"So, you agree that my butt is getting bigger," she demanded.

Lukas looked like a deer caught in headlights. "I agree you think it's getting bigger. I don't see any difference."

She huffed and pushed herself off his lap, her left hand landing squarely on the tip of his penis. He yelped like a puppy and rolled over to his side.

"What is wrong with you?"

"Nothing," he replied through clenched teeth.

"Oh, Lukas, you are such a drama queen. I think I'll try that chicken. It's smells divine!"

And just like that the fit of temper was over, and all it had cost was the first half inch of Lukas's manhood.

BY THE MIDDLE OF Emmalyn's seventh month of pregnancy, Lukas was driving her insane. He hovered incessantly and called her at least ten times a day for a status. Emmalyn loved and despised being the center of his attention.

She sighed deep in her chest as he rubbed her swollen feet and ankles one day after work. She watched the concentration on his face, and she realized just how much she loved him.

"Lukas...," she started, but his thumb was making circles on the ball of her foot and it felt too good to ignore.

"What's wrong? Am I hurting you? Do you want me to stop?" He pulled his hands away, but the murderous look in her eyes got him back to work quickly.

She rolled her eyes but smiled at him. "What do you think of moving in here with me? All the babies' stuff is here, so it would be easier for you to move in here than for us to try to find someplace else."

Lukas didn't respond, merely focused on massaging her toes, but on the inside, he was dancing with glee. " I mean, I guess that makes sense."

Emmalyn huffed. "It's okay to sound a little more enthusiastic."

He looked up from his massaging and gave her a big smile that made her tingle from her hips to her thighs. When he leaned over to kiss her, she met him half way, or as close to half way as her growing belly would allow.

The kiss between them was more than just "thank you," or even "I love you." With every swipe of his tongue and caress of her hand, it conveyed love, need, and desire. Lukas needed Emmalyn and desired her beyond reason. Emmalyn clung to his shoulders, desperate not to lose him again. When he pulled away from her, she pouted.

"We need more room." Lukas stood, pulled her off the sofa and into his arms. His mouth found hers, his lips tender yet forceful, knowing, and confident. Em's core ached, and suddenly she wanted nothing more than Lukas' hands, his mouth between her thighs, all over her body. Responding to her hunger and heeding his own, he swept her off the floor and carried her to the bedroom.

Once there, he set her on her feet, quite content to slowly and methodically undress her. She moaned every time he stopped to kiss the area he'd just uncovered. He took his time driving her mind and body wild, raining light kisses up and down her torso, then down her thighs and between her legs. She stood before him all swollen breasts and thighs and sexy belly, her lips slightly parted, her nipples hard. He couldn't remember ever seeing a more beautiful sight than Em in that moment. He simply told her, his voice thick and heavy with lust, "Lie on the bed and make sure you're comfortable. You're going to be there for a while."

And she was.

Meticulously, slowly, as though he had all the time in the world, Lukas made love to her with his hands and mouth. The wide, flat, rough surface of Lukas's tongue drove Emmalyn to the brink of madness over and over, never letting her cross into the sweetness of her passion. He used his fingers to drive in and out of Emmalyn, making her legs tremble. When he knew she'd had enough and was ready to truly cause him harm, he gave her body that one last kiss and a flick of her sensitive nub that drove her over the edge and into the arms of the orgasm she'd been building.

While she recovered her breath, he stood, removed his clothes, and lay down beside her. He was content to let her rest, but that wasn't what she had in mind. Eyes closed, he listened to her breathe and was caught completely unaware when her hand wrapped around his cock. He was so hard it was painful, and having her warm hand on him nearly caused him to spill himself. He caught her as she shifted, trying to find a comfortable position to love him as he'd loved her. Instead, she found herself being pulled onto his lap, straddling him where he'd needed it the most.

"You can do that another day. Right now, I need to be inside you," he said, his voice so gruff she could barely catch his words.

He lifted her slowly and, with equal care, lowered the woman he'd loved for so long down to sheathe him completely. He moaned with pure male satisfaction.

"You better not be going to sleep, mister," she laughed.

"I wouldn't dare."

She leaned down, catching his lower lip between her teeth. She placed her hands on his cheeks and slipped her tongue over his lips, tasting the juices she'd left on him. He tried to sit up and make things easier for her, but she put her hands on his shoulders and pushed him back down. "Nope," she said with a wicked smile. "My turn."

She shifted her knees to a position that would allow her to ride him without hurting her back. She watched the sweet pain on his face as she lifted then lowered herself in rhythm with his breathing. Emmalyn could feel the pressure building in her abdomen but didn't slow her pace. She needed this. He needed this. And they needed each other. She'd accepted that long before, but it was a driving force that gave added power to her orgasm.

Her body began to buck as Lukas held on to her and used his hips to meet her, stroke for stroke. He pulled her down for a kiss as his body released, joining her in the most earth-shattering orgasm the two had ever shared.

She wanted to stay like this, wrapped in his arms, but the pressure of the babies on her back was beginning to be the bad kind of painful. She rolled away from Lukas, and the coolness of the evening hit her. He pulled her close to him and pulled the sheet over them. They lay there, quiet, listening to the sounds of the swamp at dusk.

"I would love to move in with you, my love," he said in a whisper. He pulled his arms tighter around her. "And at the risk of ruining a perfect moment, I need to ask you something."

"You may ask me anything," she said yawning and snuggling deeper into his warmth.

"Why won't you marry me?"

She stiffened in his arms. He relaxed his hold on her just enough for her to turn over and face him.

She studied his face long enough for him to squirm under the attention. "Why is this so important to you? It wouldn't be any different from what we have now."

LORI HENDRICKS

He kissed her on the forehead and hugged her close. "Don't get mad and I know this is going to sound like male arrogance, but...I want the woman I love and my baby girls to have my name. And I want every man you meet to know that you're mine."

She nipped his chin lightly with her teeth. "You're right. That does sound arrogant, but okay," she sighed in feigned acquiescence.

Emmalyn shot Lukas a tentative look.

"Okay?" he tentatively asked.

She nodded, and he whooped with joy. Suddenly, all the stress that had been pent up in her chest released, and she laughed with a happiness she didn't think she had left in herself.

23 When Bells Toll

EMMALYN AND LUKAS ARGUED for a week about where, when, and how they were going to get married. Lukas was adamant that he didn't care, so long as it was done before the babies were born. Emmalyn was equally adamant that she did not want their wedding pictures to include her at eight months pregnant.

In the end, they settled on a courthouse wedding and a small reception, then a larger ceremony with all the bells and whistles she wanted later. There was no agreement on how long after later meant.

They did agree that though they wanted only their parents and Lukas's brother at the courthouse, they wanted their friends to be at the after party, as Lukas had taken to calling it. Lukas was in charge of corralling Delma and making sure she made it to the court-house on time. He promptly passed that duty on to his brother.

Everyone seemed excited about the wedding—except for Lukas's dad. He begrudgingly accepted his role in it, but as always, he felt Lukas was making a huge mistake. Unfortunately, he'd had the misfortune to have voiced that opinion within earshot of Delma.

"Oh, so, my daughter's not good enough for your boy," she challenged. "Well let me tell you something. You're not good enough for your boy. Ha! That's right! I said it! If you hadn't gotten in the way when they were together before, they'd have been married with three or four kids by now. But, no. What kind of father doesn't want to see his kid happy? You miserable old coot!" Her finger and face were inches away from his. Lukas had never seen Delma this fired up about anything. "You better not ruin this for them, or so help me, I'll tear you limb from limb."

Lukas's bark of laughter caught the attention of Delma's ire. He immediately righted his face, but it was too late.

"And just what, pray tell, is so funny?"

"I...Emmalyn said that exact thing to me a few weeks ago. She sounded just like you. I can't wait to tell her she sounds like her mother."

Delma's mouth twitched just enough to let Lukas know she wasn't angry. "I wouldn't do that if I were you. Things are better between my daughter and me, but she'll snap your neck if you tell her that."

Lukas looked confused. "Why? There's nothing wrong with you."

"Oh, Lukas," she said, sounding just like her daughter once more, "No girl wants to hear she's turning into her mother. Don't you know anything?"

THE AFTER PARTY WAS in full swing, and everyone was genuinely having a good time. Zavia and Isabel pulled the party together in such a short time that Lukas was genuinely surprised by everything they'd managed to do. Hosted in Zavia's spacious back yard, the food, music, and guest list were perfect.

Lukas sat off to the side and was watching Emmalyn laugh and dance with Zavia's son, Jared. His brother joined him on the deck stairs.

"She's beautiful, man. I'm so glad you got your head out of your ass."

Lukas didn't take offense. "Me too."

"Pop'll come around eventually."

"I honestly don't care at this point. I'd love for my girls to know their grandfather, but if he can't—" Lukas's voice stopped abruptly.

"What?" Jaxon watched the color drain from Lukas's face. "What's wrong?" he asked to Lukas's back.

Emmalyn had fallen down, and she wasn't moving. Lukas ran over to her and dropped to his knees by her side. She was conscious, but her eyes looked crazy. She grabbed his hand.

"I think the babies are coming," she moaned.

"Call an ambulance!" he yelled to no one and everyone. "Hold on Emmy. We'll get you to the hospital."

The tears fell from Emmalyn's eyes. "It's too early…." She screamed as another contraction tore through her. She squeezed his hand, and with a painful snap, she'd broken the bone.

"Emmalyn!"

"The pains started yesterday, but I thought they were Braxton Hicks pains, not actual contractions. The doctor said they were normal, but this is different," she said breathlessly.

"Get her into the house," Delma said. "Zee, where is a good place to wait for the ambulance?"

"Take her to the living room," Zavia said. Scared to death, she took a step back as Lukas hoisted Emmalyn into his arms and turned to carry her into the house. Zavia covered her mouth to hold on to a scream as she saw the huge bloodstain Em left on the patio. Isabel grabbed on to her and began to cry.

"That's not good. They need to get her to the hospital now!" Isabel whispered harshly.

Just as Zavia made her way to the living room, the sound of sirens could be heard approaching the house from a distance. She sent Jared and Robert out to the street to flag down the EMTs. They returned a few minutes later.

"What's the situation?" asked one of the EMTs. Lukas repeated what Em had told him and about the blood stain on the patio. The EMT knelt down beside Emmalyn and began taking vitals. "Her pulse is weak," he said over his shoulder to his partner. "We need to get her to the hospital."

The two men worked to get Emmalyn on the gurney.

"How far along is she?" asked the second EMT.

"Thirty-six weeks," Lukas replied. His knees gave out on him when he saw Emmalyn's blood on the sofa cushions. His father and brother helped him stand.

"You need to ride with her, Lukas," Delma pointed out. "And you need to hold it together. She can't be any more scared than she is right now. Be her rock."

Lukas nodded. He followed the EMTs and his new wife out of the house. It took him two tries to pull himself into the back of the ambulance.

LUKAS, EMMALYN, TWO DOCTORS, and a slew of nurses had been in the delivery room for almost three hours before the first baby was born. He'd expected hours and hours of labor, but this one came out surprisingly fast. The doctors were huddled over the baby, checking her over. Prematurely born babies could have so many issues, Lukas remembered from his and Em's prenatal classes.

The shorter of the two doctors kept looking over his shoulder at Emmalyn and frowning. Lukas was just about ready to demand that they tell them what was wrong with his daughter when Emmalyn screamed, not the scream of someone in pain but a scared and frustrated scream. The sound stunned everyone in the room, including the baby, who began to cry in earnest.

Then, one of the machines began to beep angrily, followed by another. Emmalyn's blood pressure was spiking. Lukas bent down and kissed his new wife on the forehead. It was hot yet clammy feeling. Lukas looked to the doctors hoping someone had an answer. One of the nurses came around to his side of the bed and tried to usher Lukas out of the room.

"I'm not leaving my wife," he protested.

"Make sure they save the baby," Emmalyn exhaled. She didn't have much voice left and zero energy. "Whatever happens, make sure they save Gia." The words ended on a moan and the sound of water splashing. She gripped his hand with a strength that surprised them both. Her eyes clouded over as wave after wave of pain tore through her. Her color drained.

"Emmalyn, I need you." He didn't want to say it aloud, but he'd sacrifice just about anyone to keep Em by his side.

"Swear it to me, Lukas. I need to know my girls will be okay, or all this will have been for nothing."

"All of what?" Lukas looked at Emmalyn as if she'd lost her mind. Of course he would save Emmalyn. He'd love his kids, but he needed Em as much as he needed air or water. She was the strong one, the responsible one. He couldn't raise two little girls by himself.

"Sir, we need to get your wife prepped for surgery. You need to leave so we can try to save her life." The nurse forcefully pulled Lukas's hand from Em's death grip, pushing him toward the doors.

"For a little thing she was very strong," he thought somewhere in his mind. Then the nurse's words sank in and he rounded on her, causing her to pause for the briefest of moments before pushing him out the door completely.

"Save her? What the fuck do you mean save her? Emmalyn!" As he stumbled out, he saw the puddle of blood on the floor beneath Emmalyn's legs. Two security guards were waiting outside the room for him. They each grabbed an arm and pulled him away from his wife and daughters toward the waiting room where eight concerned family and friends waited. What was he going to say? His knees buckled, and nothing in him could stop the free fall.

"Lukas, what's wrong?" Delma was on him before he hit the ground. He was in shock.

"Lukas, how is Emmy? Where are the babies?" This question came from Zavia.

He looked up at Delma and Zavia, saw the joy and hope in their eyes. It broke him. "I don't know," he croaked out. He wasn't able to get air in his lungs. A strong slap to the face brought him out of his misery, and his anger to the surface.

"Damn it, Lukas, snap out of it. Where are Emmalyn and the babies?" Delma yelled.

"I. Don't. Know," Lukas ground out between clenched teeth. He staggered to his feet, walked over to the row of chairs, and slumped down into the first one he came to. He leaned over in the seat, his head cradled in his hands. He didn't have the strength to fight the tears. "She's lost a lot of blood. She birthed one of the twins, but the other wasn't coming. Ava. She named her Ava. She asked me to make sure they saved Gia. The nurse...the nurse said they have to get Emmy to the OR to try to save her."

Delma fainted. Brian and Isabel helped her up and over to a chair.

"Save her? Save Emmalyn you mean?" Isabel asked, jaw trembling from fighting the urge to cry out.

"That's what they said," Lukas replied. His chest ached as did his hand. He looked down and saw that his knuckles had swollen and were beginning to turn blue. Somewhere in his mind was a vague memory of Em squeezing his hand and snapping the bone.

No one spoke for what seemed to be an eternity. Delma had snapped awake, but merely cried softly on

Brian's shoulder. What could any of them say? There were no words of comfort for any of them.

A nurse came out after some time, holding a tiny pink bundle. "Mr. Upton? Would you like to hold your daughter?"

Lukas couldn't move. Neither could Delma. The nurse looked at him in understanding. Zavia walked over to the nurse and peeked into the bundle. She barely backed away before the sobs hit.

"She looks just like Emmy," was all she could get out before crying in earnest. She turned to her husband and buried her face against his shoulder. Robert held on to his wife as her grief washed over her.

"Please ask someone to give Mr. Upton and Mrs. Upton's mother an update," Robert asked softly. "The wait is killing them."

The nurse nodded and stepped back into the area where the rooms were. She stopped at the door and turned back to Lukas. "Ava will be in the nursery when you're ready, Mr. Upton."

No one asked about the second baby. They didn't think they needed to.

Another two hours passed before the short doctor, of the worried face and harried whispers, stepped into the waiting room. Lukas took one look at the man's face and knew.

"I'm very sorry, Mr. Upton. We weren't able to save your wife or your second daughter, Gia. We realized too late that Gia's umbilical cord was wrapped around her neck. She was stillborn when we removed her after performing the emergency C-section. At your wife's insistence, we did attempt to save Gia.

"Your wife had lost a lot of blood. It would appear that she had been bleeding for some time. Her body was very weak and couldn't take the trauma. I take it she didn't say anything to you about the trouble she's been having?" He paused and looked around at the people in the room. "So much grief," he thought.

"No. She didn't say a word," Lukas whispered. His brain had stopped functioning. All he needed now was for his heart to stop beating. "I can't understand it. People have babies everyday."

"I'm very sorry, sir. Your wife had gestational diabetes, which resulted in pre-eclampsia. At some point over the last few weeks, she developed eclampsia. The bleeding was a symptom of her elevated blood pressure. If she had checked herself into the hospital sooner, we could have possibly saved her and the second baby. Her doctor—"

Lukas cut him off with a roar and a new bout of tears. "She told me she'd had her last doctor's appointment two weeks ago, and now we were just waiting for the babies to come. I didn't know, didn't question it."

The doctor sighed as he understood more about what happened. He hated this part of the job. "I would bet your wife was told to have the babies earlier to reduce the strain on her body. Any doctor worth his degree would have recommended that." He waited for Lukas to regain control of himself. The poor man was grief stricken and dumbfounded. He didn't blame Lukas. Any man would have reacted the same to finding that his wife had scarified herself to give the babies a better chance at survival. "Ava will be ready to be discharged in a couple of days. She's basically a healthy baby girl, very lucky indeed. You will need to work with her on her breathing, and the nurses will explain exactly what needs to be done."

"Can I see her?" Lukas asked as the doctor turned to go back to the maternity ward.

"Ava?"

"No. Emmalyn. Can I see her?"

The doctor nodded in understanding. "I'll make the arrangements," he replied.

The doctor turned and walked away from the broken man and the people who'd loved the woman he'd spent the last several hours trying to save. He couldn't understand why the woman hadn't told anyone about how sick she was. It should have been enough to cause anyone concern. The situation quickly zipped out of his mind as another round of alarms went off, signaling a new emergency.

LUKAS COULDN'T LOOK AT the woman lying on the bed and equate her with the woman he'd married earlier that day. And he absolutely couldn't look into the small crib that sat to the bed's immediate right. He slipped quietly into the room and sat at the foot of the bed, the stark silence of the room a testament to lack of life.

"This isn't how it's supposed to be, Emmy. You're supposed to be here. We're supposed to do this together. You promised we'd be a family, and now you're gone. What am I going to do?" he asked the silence in desperation. "I can't take care of Ava without you."

His grief overcame him with the force of a tractor trailer. Lukas folded over and cried until there wasn't a tear left in his body. His head ached terribly, but he couldn't bring himself to leave the room.

Jaxon, Pop, and Delma watched quietly from outside the room. Each was lost in thought, though all of those thoughts centered around Lukas, Emmalyn, and Ava.

Jaxon wanted to go to his brother and offer support, though he had no idea what to say. It wasn't going to be okay. Nothing was going to be all right about this situation. He turned and walked back to the waiting room, unable to deal with the pain that was storming in that hospital room.

Delma had stopped to check on Ava on the way to say goodbye to her daughter. The baby looked just like Emmalyn, same dark hair, same perfect brown skin, same wise, knowing eyes. Delma's chest felt like she'd been kicked. She wanted to help Lukas, but the weight of her own grief was draining her. She turned to leave as well, not able to face her daughter's body, nor that of her dead granddaughter. Before she walked away, she turned to Pop.

With malice and hatred vibrating in her voice she said, "If you say a single thing against my daughter to that boy in there or to my granddaughter, you won't live to regret the choice. Count on that."

POP ENTERED THE ROOM, intent on nothing but ushering his son to the nursery. He couldn't stop himself from creeping deeper into the room and peering in at Gia, the second twin. She looked so beautiful and peaceful lying there. Emmalyn's face was pale and gaunt, likely from the loss of blood. He quickly turned to Lukas, who'd risen from his seat and was prepared to fight.

"Going to tell me that you told me so," Lukas challenged.

"No, son. I was going to take you to visit your daughter. She needs you." Pop took a step back, frightened by the violence and grief in his son's eyes.

Lukas's shoulders slumped, all the fight gone from him. "I...I can't, not yet." Lukas unwillingly looked down at Em's body. His shoulders shook, but he didn't make a sound.

Pop reached up and pulled Lukas's face toward him. "Yes, you can. And you have to. Ava is completely innocent in all this, and she needs the love of her father. The bond may not happen right away, but a day will come when Ava will be everything in the world to you. And it will be enough. I swear it."

"How can you be so sure?"

"Because I had that moment with you and your brother after your mother killed herself. I refused to accept it because I missed that woman so much it burned in my skin. In that refusal, I turned into a hard bitter old man, who wouldn't know good luck or fortune if it bit me on the nose. I can't let that happen to you. You're right—Emmalyn was not like your mother. Em would never have left you, no matter what you'd done.

"I know it won't happen now, but you'll be given a chance to open your heart to that little girl, and when it happens, you have to take it, for both of your sakes."

"She's gone, Pop. She's gone."

"I know. And you're going to grieve more than you think you're capable of. But right now, you need to go hold your daughter."

Lukas nodded and followed his father out of the room, unable to turn for one last look at the only light in his life.

24 EPILOGUE

LITTLE AVA HAD HER mother's eyes. Two years later and Lukas still had the hardest time looking into his baby girl's chocolate-brown eyes. He and Emmalyn were supposed to have the happy ending, but life had a funny way of getting in the way of the fairy tale. He missed his Emmy endlessly. After her death, Lukas honestly believed he would never recover. He didn't want to eat, sleep, or even to live without Emmy on this earth.

The pain was more than he thought he'd ever be able to live through despite putting one foot in front of the other each day. Yet every night he saw Emmalyn's face that day in the hospital, begging him to save the baby, even if it meant losing her. Every morning, he'd lie in bed with his eyes closed for an extra second and pray that it was all a mistake and Emmy would be there holding Ava and Gia. Every morning he turned over, her side of the bed was empty, and the grieving process would begin again.

Because he was so lost in his grief, Lukas's mother-in-law had moved back east to look after Ava for a while. However, the grief Delma felt seeing her lost daughter in her granddaughter's eyes became too much. She railed at him to get it together and care for his child, the child his wife—her daughter—had sacrificed her life for.

Then his father and brother stepped in for several months to help. Jaxon put off his next assignment to stay with his brother and try to help Lukas with his grief. Eventually, Jaxon talked Lukas into going back to Charleston to clean out the apartment he and Emmalyn had shared. At their apartment, he went through every piece of paper Emmalyn had saved.

Right after the funeral, he'd reached out to Em's doctors to get the truth of what she'd been hiding from him. The pregnancy had been difficult from the start, and it had been recommended that Em terminate the pregnancy or at the very least stop working and focus on her health. The doctor went through it all—the gestational diabetes, the endless fatigue, her inability to eat and gain weight, the pre-eclampsia. She told him that at thirty weeks she had recommended a C-section to Emmalyn, and to let the girls try to survive outside the womb. She'd told Emmalyn that her body couldn't survive another ten weeks of carrying the twins.

She'd known. She'd known all along, and she never said anything to him. It was his fault for not being there at the appointments. Lukas could see Em wasn't well, but he too easily wrote it off as normal pregnancy woes. But he couldn't quite understand why she would risk all that she was, her life, to carry those babies. He would have given her anything in the world she ever wanted. It wasn't like he couldn't afford it, but she didn't trust him enough to ask for help. He'd live with that guilt for the rest of his life.

While packing, he found the box Emmy had with every letter he'd written her, every trinket he'd ever bought her, even every ticket stub for every movie they'd seen together. It was all he could do to close the box and put it back in the closet. He was tired of crying and couldn't take the memories those items evoked. He would ask Zavia and Isabel to hold on to those things until Ava was ready to know about her parents' courtship.

In time, the physical pain in his chest and his broken hand faded. The pain of the memories would take a lot longer to fade, but he was determined that Ava would know what an amazing woman her mother was. Lukas would eventually look back at the man he was and appreciate the man he had become. He knew things had happened as they were meant to, but he couldn't help but be sad about the family that could have been and the life he'd always dreamed of with the woman he loved by his side.

THEN THE DAY HIS father had sworn would come had finally come. Lukas finally looked at Ava and understood what Emmy had fought for, this beautiful little girl with a quick laugh and endless energy, just like her mother. And he knew his love for his lost love would be supplemented by the boundless love he had for his daughter. He watched Ava playing in her room. She smiled up at him brightly, and for the first time in a long time, he found his smile.

His daughter's shining smile was a constant reminder to Lukas of his Emmy, and he couldn't stop himself from falling a little more in love with Ava every day.

ACKNOWLEDGEMENTS

I want to thank everyone who helped me write and publish my first romance novel. It was a long road and I am ever so appreciative of the support and advice I have received along the way.

In specific, I want to thank **Madhuri Blaylock** for beta reading and giving me pointers on how to spice my story up. You are an amazing writer and an awesome person, and you don't know how much I appreciate your help. If you haven't read her books, you simply must check them out!

ABOUT THE AUTHOR

Lori Hendricks is an IT project manager by day and novelist by night. A longtime lover of words, she reads science fiction, fantasy and paranormal romance novels regularly (when there is time). When not reading, writing or working, Lori can most often be found watching football or basketball with her adorable cat, Mona